THE URBANA FREE LIBRARY
W9-BCD-441

THE URBANA FREE LIBRARY
TO RENEW MATERIALS CALL
(217) 367-4057

THE RED THREAD

紅

絲

THE RED THREAD

A LOVE STORY

by Nicholas Jose

CHRONICLE BOOKS
SAN FRANCISCO

This is a work of fiction. Names, places, characters, and incidents are products of the author's imagination or are used fictionally. Any resemblance to actual people, places, or events is entirely coincidental.

Library of Congress Cataloging-in-Publication Data:

Jose, Nicholas, 1952-
The red thread : a love story / Nicholas Jose.
256 p. 14 x 20.3 cm.
ISBN 0-8118-2951-0
1. Shanghai (China)–Fiction. I. Title.

PR9619.3.J73 R44 2000
823'.914–dc21 00-024082

Printed in the United States
Designed by Laura Lovett
Calligraphy by Jianwei Fong
Typeset by Peter Kesselman in Berthold Baskerville and John Handy

Published in Australia by Hardie Grant Books
12 Claremont Street
South Yarra
3141 Australia

Distributed in Canada by Raincoast Books
9050 Shaughnessy Street
Vancouver, British Columbia V6P 6E5

10 9 8 7 6 5 4 3 2 1

Chronicle Books LLC
85 Second Street
San Francisco, California 94105
www.chroniclebooks.com

For Claire

樂

1.

WEDDED BLISS

An old man steps off a ferry at the docks on a chilly winter afternoon. Weng is tall and gaunt, and stooped, carrying his bag not by the handles but cradled in his arms like a baby. His face is peanut-shaped, swelling at the cranium, narrow at the ears and wide again at the jaw and chin. His skin is tight, almost translucent. His thick glasses, hanging from his ears, wobble on his low nose. The old-style collar of his padded jacket is buttoned at the neck. In dusty cotton shoes he treads gently on the ribbed ramp that crosses from the boat to the labyrinth of barriers that leads the way out.

For the greater part of a century Weng has carried himself with the demeanor of a scholar, bowing his head to the task at hand, sticking to tedious clerical work in the backroom–copying down records, sorting files–while political tumult howled fire and ice outside. This way he has survived with his wits about him to become Old Weng. He has lived to indulge his deepest impulse, the understanding of old things–to handle them, collect them, deal in them. It is the passion that runs in his veins and defines his life.

The tea in his jar has gone bitter now. Hungry and weary after the journey downstream from his hometown, he is excited nevertheless to be arriving in Shanghai. His step has an extra pulse of energy and his eyes glint as he approaches a pedicab man who is sitting with his feet on the pedals ready to go. Old Weng bargains the man down. The man boasts that in the course of the day the tray on the back of the pedicab has already carted a computer system in many boxes, a tub of live crabs, tight-bound piles of magazines, and an assortment of passengers.

Now it carries Old Weng, who crouches over the bag in his lap, his legs dangling.

The city that enchanted him as a young man has changed almost beyond recognition, yet somehow the atmosphere remains the same, as if some of the ghosts have stayed on. The sunset glow seems to make the wide river melt into the dark coppery sky just as he remembers. Boat lights, vaguely disembodied, make steady tracks. Fairy lights twinkle in scalloped strings along the waterfront as the buildings light up at the end of the working day, the grand old edifices of imperial stone dwarfed by the glass façades of a new economic empire, projecting ever upward.

The pedicab creeps along at street level, weaving through the bustle, turning down a narrow lane, cutting through to another grand, crowded thoroughfare. Old Weng climbs down outside Shanghai's newest, tallest tower and pays the fare. The automatic doors of the building open and shut like the mouth of a puffing fish, letting him in. Seeing his reflection in the sliding screens of glass as he goes inside, dreaming of his youth, the old man almost fails to recognize himself. Then he makes his way across the sea of green marble to the elevator.

Gold letters shadowed in black spell out the name on the door of an office on the forty-first floor: *Shanghai Art Auctions International.* The jaw-doors open again for Old Weng and he enters the pool of cold halogen light where the desks float, empty, and all the computer screens but one are dark.

He squeezes the bag in his arms.

"Young Shen," the old man said warmly as the young man came forward to greet him.

"You must be tired," Shen replied, courteously, with a touch on the elbow, leading the visitor to an armchair by the window. "Tea?" he said, fetching two mugs of tea and setting them down on the low table. The old man removed his woolen cap and warmed his hands around the mug. He removed the lid and raised the tea to his lips, blowing the dark leaves across the steaming surface before putting down the mug and waiting for the leaves to settle, as was his custom.

Brightness played over Shen's face as he nodded appreciatively at his visitor's old-fashioned way.

"How old are you now?" the old man asked.

"Thirty this year," Shen replied.

"San shi er li," commented Old Weng. "The age Confucius says a person should settle their affairs."

In time, perhaps, Shen's head would grow into the same shape as Old Weng's. For now Shen's cheeks were chubby and his face had a molded look, as if a potter had shaped it. His skin was pale. His hair was black and shiny as raven's wings. He could not help his eagerness as he pointed out the space on the table where the old man should unpack his things.

Old Weng tugged at the zipper to open the canvas bag. The first parcel was tightly wrapped in layers of newspaper and crisscrossed with knotted string that he painstakingly untied. Young Shen watched impatiently. One layer of newsprint after another was peeled away, like the skins of an onion, until the object appeared. It was a celadon ewer with a good, rich glaze. Old Weng turned it in his hands. It was several centuries old but had no reign mark. It must have come from a rustic kiln and was very good of its kind. Rough, rather scarce. The celadon was a smoky green, like cloud reflected in turbid water. It was, in any case, only a chaser.

Shen, who had been hovering, sat down at last in the chair opposite Old Weng, allowing the veteran collector to take his time.

From even more layers of paper the next parcel revealed an unblemished piece of blanc de chine. It was a small figure of a woman, slender and turning, her eyes downcast, with one hand nestling a pearl in her lap and the other held against her heart in a gesture of blessing. The glaze was pearly, white as snow yet shimmering like gauzy sunlight.

"Guanyin," said Shen, identifying her as the Goddess of Compassion. One bare foot poked forward from where she stood in the heart of a lotus that floated like a boat in curling wavelets.

"Dehua-ware," confirmed the old man with a nod, locating the kiln and by inference the dynasty, Ming, from which the piece came.

"Very fine," Shen observed, running his finger over the delicate modeling.

The old man smiled with pride, fully aware of what he had, not merely the object but the connoisseurship required to recognize it too. He casually handed it to Shen, who took it between his palms and rotated it, admiring the detailing of drapery and jewels.

Then, as if in an afterthought, Old Weng pointed out the mark that identified the maker by name. "He Chaozhong," he said. He was the most renowned maker of all. But by then Old Weng was already untangling the string from the next parcel, his nimble fingers producing a deep red bowl that he upended to show the reign mark of the Qianlong Emperor on the base. The bowl had such presence and authority that it simply *was,* and at the same time it seemed to center the whole open-plan office of Shanghai Art Auctions International. A spectacular piece, its oxblood glaze, like liquid garnet, absorbing the strange light of this world, three centuries remote from the time when it was made, as it reflected the faces of the two men who peered into it.

Shen put the blanc de chine Guanyin on the table and, with a nod of permission from the old man, let his fingers reach for the bowl that the Emperor himself must have praised. It was neither hot nor cold to the touch. It felt glossy, almost viscous. “Not bad,” Shen grinned. He felt a ripple up his spine as beneath the glaze he deciphered the veiled pattern of a dragon in the clouds.

He got his pad and calculator.

While Shen was working out prices, Old Weng steadily opened the last of the parcels. This one was rectangular, wrapped in two layers of newsprint from the *People's Daily* and an inner layer of brown paper. It contained a book that was bound traditionally in several loose stitchings that were sandwiched between red cloth boards and fastened with red silk ribbons, two on each side. Old Weng untied the little bows and presented Shen with the first of the four slim bindings that made up the book. The characters on the title page were woodblock-printed: large, chunky, and black as soot. *Six Chapters of a Floating Life,* Shen read out. Of which this was Chapter One.

He turned the first page. The print ran in regular spaced columns. Words caught his eye. Flower names. Boats.

“It's the earliest printing,” explained Old Weng.

Shen picked up each of the separately bound chapters in turn. “Only four?” he asked.

“Ah!” sighed the collector, his lips curling back to reveal the gaps in his teeth. “The last two chapters are missing.”

“Missing?”

“Lost. They've never been found.”

"Never?" Shen looked up with interest. "You mean the book was never finished."

"It was never published in the author's lifetime," the old man explained. "The final chapters may have gone missing from the author's papers or may have got lost on the way to the printer or may never have been written after all. He wrote only for himself and his friends. It's an account of his life."

"What was his name?"

"Shen Fu."

"Shen–like me?"

"That's right. It's the same character."

The old man chuckled as the younger man looked more intently at the book, holding it so tightly in his hands that for a moment the pages seemed to grow from the tips of his fingers, the paper a layer of his skin that had been stamped and peeled away. Shen tried some lines from the opening page on his tongue, doing his best to decipher the formal language, then he looked into the old man's eyes in wonder.

"I can feel it drawing me in," he said.

Since the *Book of Songs* begins with a poem about wedded bliss, I will begin this account by speaking of my marital relations and let other matters follow. My only regret is that I was not properly educated in childhood. All I know is a simple language and I shall try only to record the real facts and real sentiments. I hope the reader will be kind enough not to scrutinize my wording. That would be like looking for brilliance in a tarnished mirror.

Old Weng smiled, looking at Shen with the vital gloss of

young manhood still on his skin. "It is a love story," he said good-humoredly.

Shen exhaled deeply. Love? He did not know if he had ever experienced it. Beauty, yes, the intense beauty of perfectly created objects–but that, he suspected, was not love. He inserted the four chapters neatly between the red boards, tied the four red ribbons, and handed the book back.

He began writing figures in pencil on the pad. The auction house took a commission of 15 percent from the vendor and another 10 percent from the buyer over and above the hammer price. The estimates had to be in line with the market, a little higher to indicate quality, but not so high as to frighten off bargain hunters. The eventual selling price, however, need bear no relation to the estimate, which was chiefly a benchmark to print in the catalog, a piece of bait to dangle.

In the old days when the trade was forbidden, the risks high, covert dealers like the old man had been forced to take what they could get. Now with the market open and rich Overseas Chinese ready to pay to recover a part of their heritage, prices had soared. The celadon was scarce. The Guanyin was rare. The oxblood bowl was more than rare–it was unique. They settled on high reserve prices for all three. The old man found the figures diverting. He would never in several lifetimes have had so much money to spend himself. But all those zeroes missed the point. The pieces did cost time and money and alertness, the exchange of favors and a lifelong pursuit of stray threads. But the value of treasured pieces was ultimately a quality of the civilization that made them, a chance excellence with the power to travel forward into the future, intensifying as it went.

The book was different, though. A first edition was an item for specialists only. It did not speak for itself beyond language in the way the bowl did. It needed to be passed on through the hands of those who, in reading it, would appreciate it properly. It could not just sit on a shelf. The estimate they agreed on for the book had three zeroes less than for the bowl—and even there Shen admitted he was flying blind. He knew very little about old books. Four chapters of a book of six chapters. A minor literati classic, a memoir. They agreed it was a curiosity.

They chatted under the bright white light, just the two of them drinking tea among the filing cabinets and computer terminals of the spacious office. Shen's American boss had left early, as usual, leaving Shen to lock up. Refilling their mugs with hot water, Shen knew enough not to pry into Old Weng's trade secrets. Old Weng managed to find extraordinary things deep in the hinterland of the southern country and he was unerring in his assessments. Shen recognized himself as part of the system of flow and exchange, part of the circulation of timeless objects. He was pleased to be admitted to Old Weng's domain in that way.

The old man folded the official receipt from the auction company into the inside pocket of his padded jacket, resettled his glasses on his ears and stood up. He was tall even with his stoop, but the curve of his spine made him seem to be bowing to the yoke. Perhaps, in an abstracted way, although he operated strictly by himself, implicating no one else, he served the past rather than the present and carried the burden of all those fallen dynasties. He was repaid by the livelihood their old glories provided him, a steady trickle with large sums on rare occasions but never enough to make him do away with his cloth shoes. It was understanding, not money, that he accrued.

Carefully he packed away the used paper and string in his bag. "Till next time," he said, shaking young Shen's hand as they parted at the elevator. Then he was off in search of a hole in the wall down an unlit lane where he could eat spiced peanuts and chicken and drink yellow wine.

Shen rewrapped the three ceramics in bubble plastic and locked them in the safe. He looked at his watch. The time for eating had almost passed. He ran his fingers through his hair, then he sat down in the chair where the old collector had sat and found a cigarette. His hand reached for the book. He peered at the columns of text through a blur of smoke and a curtain of hair until his vision jumped into focus and he could read the literary words.

I was born in the year 1763, in the reign of the Qianlong Emperor, when the country was prosperous and at peace. I knew great joys and great sorrows, but, as the poet says, our life is little more than a spring daydream, and in a moment all is vanished forever. My name is Shen Fu, the son of a humble country administrator.

And my name is Shen Fuling, thought Shen, and I am a member of the same great clan as you. While I was studying in America, I took the name of Sean, after the actor who played James Bond, because it was easier to adopt a foreign name. Otherwise people avoided calling you by any name at all, in case they got it wrong. Without a name they might soon forget your existence altogether. So I became Sean. Sean Shen. Like Sean Penn, people would ask. The movie star? Yeah, that's right.

My English was already good when I graduated from Fudan University in Shanghai. After my time at college I spoke like a native, only with greater consciousness of changes in register. My father, Professor Shen, was on the committee for academic exchanges between China and the United States. He is a distinguished historian of modern China and a leading Communist Party intellectual. As a dialectical materialist, he knew that global capitalism would triumph over all other ideologies and systems in the late twentieth century and that by harnessing those energies China would grow rich and preeminent once again. In that way he is still a revolutionary. He planned for me, his firstborn son, to become an economist and an American green card holder, an analyst of money flow for the transnational corporations that were extending their operations into China. It was his string-pulling that got me into the turbocharged economics program at Georgetown University, along with all those jocks and nerds and geniuses, the sons and daughters of Washington lawyers and Wall Street traders.

That was when I became addicted to television, French fries, the Colonel, chocolate chip ice cream, pad Thai noodles. I worked out at the gym and developed muscle. I wore my campus sweatshirt with pride. But underneath I always remained a studious young gentleman from Shanghai.

On weekends I educated myself by visiting the city museum. It had a rich collection of Classical sculpture, medieval and Renaissance manuscripts, eighteenth- and nineteenth-century European painting, and American art from early folk craft through to the most contemporary installations. It rewarded me in ways that my economics studies failed to do. The museum also had an important oriental collection that included a traditional Chinese house plundered by a Yankee adventurer and removed to the States when China was on her knees in the late Qing dynasty. Inside that house a scholar's studio was set up replete with the finest old brush holder, ink-mixing bowl, and calligraphic scrolls. The objects were impossibly distanced from the life of their own culture, but respected there in that foreign environment to a degree I had never seen before.

There was one particular tea bowl in one of the glass cases to which I became quite attached. It was a rather inconspicuous bowl of a brown-gray color that appeared in hairline streaks, sometimes chestnut brown, sometimes ash gray–or the gray of faded cloth shoes, maybe with olive or a touch of violet in it. The glaze was named hare's fur for the crystalline lines that formed when the iron in the black pigment was fired at a certain temperature. The bowl was one to hold in your hand, although in the museum you were not allowed to do that. I checked it every time I went there, as if the bowl belonged to me. I suppose, in the isolation of my student life, that bowl of hare's-fur glaze was one of my few close associates. Thus I came to realize that my own culture lay hidden deep within me and that it would require work on my part to gain access to it.

The other piece that fascinated me was a stone head of the Buddha that came from a monastery at Mount Lu, far up the Yangtze River. The face with three-quarter-closed eyes was utterly quiet. That head, carved a thousand years ago, had been sawn off and souvenired by a booty collector. Somewhere out there was the headless body, a butchered trunk, dumbly awaiting the return of its graceful head. Maybe that was something I could do, put the missing parts together.

My visits to the museum made me change my mind about economics. I had complied out of filial piety, but I was not interested in following my shrewd old father's path to wealth and influence. I could never discipline my mind to the dry speculation of economics. I knew myself for what I was–a dabbler, a dilettante, susceptible to every kind of distraction.

A curator in the oriental department of the museum befriended me at that time. She was glad to have a visitor with whom to share her enthusiasms. She helped me transfer to the graduate program in art history. With only one economics semester to my credit–in which I learnt the idea of the unbendable laws of the marketplace–I was now able to devote myself to the study of beautiful things. My father was furious. He said I was a vain and selfish idiot, and from that day on he put all his hopes of restoring the family's fortunes in my younger brother, Fuming, who was supposed to have a head for business.

But I was happy, and being happy I excelled. Even before

I graduated I was headhunted by a new auction house that was setting up in Shanghai in direct competition with the big international names. With all the right credentials–fluent English, a good American graduate degree, and a nose for Chinese antiquities–I found myself back in my hometown working for Shanghai Art Auctions International.

Settle your life at thirty, Confucius says. *San shi er li.* Get married. Make a home.

Well, I was to take another path.

Shen smoked the last of his cigarette and put down the book. The old Chinese literary language of the text was slow-going, half-classical, half-vernacular of two hundred years ago, slow but exquisitely pleasurable, as if in small polite steps he was being admitted to the private world of Shen Fu, to a chamber of the heart where the innermost memories unfolded, the most intimate confessions.

Reading a page a day in his spare moments, Shen took a couple of weeks to finish the first chapter, which was entitled "Wedded Bliss." By that time the catalog for the forthcoming auction had been printed and the viewing was due to begin. Reluctantly he let the book go.

✻ ✻ Shanghai Art Auctions International rented the elaborately refurbished ballroom of the prerevolutionary French club for the viewing. The oval plaster ceiling was festooned with snowy stucco garlands and windows of art nouveau stained glass, and the original curving staircase with its ornate ironwork banister swept up from the foyer. The new Japanese management had agreed to preserve the ballroom as part of a deal to obtain possession of the prime downtown site for a five-star hotel. But despite the splendor of the room, Shen felt glum. Atop a white plinth that was far too big, the book labeled *Six Chapters of a Floating Life* sat in sorry isolation in its red covers. No one even stopped to pick it up. It was out of place in an auction of fine and decorative arts. In any case, Shen did not like being separated from the book before he had finished reading it.

As viewers drifted through, Shen sat at the information desk and fielded inquiries, registering those who intended to bid. Ricky, his young English colleague, sat beside him and gossiped. Ricky Chittleborough had an Oxford-educated knowledge of Chinese culture, but his judgment of antiques was hit and miss. He had white-blond hair and a rhinestone stud in his ear, and a cheerfully sarcastic manner that made him seem streetwise. Before he joined the auction house, Ricky had made money by taking tourists through Shanghai's antiques markets. He knew how to convince people they were getting the better end of a deal. As a foreigner he was paid a higher salary than Shen, even though his English was actually no better. He was an asset for the company with the foreign community, particularly the European buyers, who never really trusted Chinese.

Shen and Ricky liked to joke with each other. Shen had trouble pronouncing Ricky's surname–Chittleborough was a mouthful–and called him Ricky Chitty instead. Ricky burnt the candle at both ends. When he and Shen ate together after work, Ricky would always suggest places to go on to, a bar or a nightclub or a rendezvous with some larger-than-life group. As a well-bred Shanghainese, Shen had nothing much to say to most of Ricky's associates, not wishing to be acquainted with them himself, but he was happy to go clubbing with Ricky. Shen kept himself aloof, then late into the night, when he was drunk, he relaxed among the sloe-eyed girls and boys of some sleazy bar where the atmosphere was all smoke and warmth and joking laughter. The next morning at work Ricky would tease him and say that slumming was his natural element.

"Watch out, here comes Linda," said Ricky.

Linda Hummel, their boss's wife, was American Chinese, from a family that fled Shanghai in 1949 when the Communists took over. Her husband, Stanley, had been working in the company's head office in Houston, Texas, when the plan was hatched to expand into China. Linda paraded her Shanghai connections in front of the chief executive and Stanley was given the job of setting up the new branch–so Stanley liked to explain, giving his wife the credit she deserved. He and Linda worked as a team. Their mission was to make Shanghai Art Auctions International the only game in town within five years.

"Hi, guys," Linda said, hurrying over to the desk where Shen and Ricky were sitting. Her hair was lacquered in a shell shape and she wore a jade-green suit that made her skin look slightly green too. "Guess what?" she whispered, leaning forward and checking over her shoulder for spies. "According to my niece Ivy, the Deputy Mayor has expressed an interest in attending the auction. Oh, I do hope he can make it. I'm working on Ivy." Linda rubbed two fingers together. "Ivy's like this with the Deputy Mayor's private secretary. You've met Ivy, haven't you, Sean? Not only beautiful, but so clever."

Shen hated it when Linda called him Sean. It showed she was uncomfortable with Chinese names, even though she was Chinese. And as for Ivy, thought Shen, even apart from the name, Linda had one too many of these so-called nieces who worked for her and in return expected help in their quest for potential husbands. If Shen married anyone, Linda had decided, it must be one of her nieces. She could not let him go to waste.

"Yes," said Linda, turning her back on Ricky. He was a bad influence on Shen as far as she was concerned. "Ivy's thick as thieves with Mr. Zhang Jun from the Deputy Mayor's office and she says he is so interested in art. Oh, that gorgeous lacquer screen"–now she faced Ricky accusingly–"don't you think it needs more light?"

The screen depicted a pair of brilliant blue-and-green peacocks among red and white camellias on a golden ground. "People might pass out just from looking at it," Ricky said sardonically.

"It's a question of balance," said Shen, the diplomat.

"You guys are the experts," laughed Linda, unconvinced, as she went to find Stanley.

Stanley Hummel was pleased with the number of people who attended the viewing. The mail-out had been a success. People came from Beijing, Hong Kong, Taipei, from Europe and North America. But he knew that a new company would be judged on the professionalism of the sale and on the prices they achieved. Linda had found an experienced local man to call the auction, but to make doubly sure things went smoothly, Stanley was also flying in a top auctioneer from the head office. Then the day before the sale, the fellow called from Houston and canceled, and Stanley was stuck.

"Get one of our own boys to do it," said Linda. "It's a training opportunity for Sean."

So Stanley asked Shen, and, since his boss was doing him a favor, Shen had no choice but to agree.

✷ ✷ A banner looped across the stage hailed THE FIRST INTERNATIONAL SHANGHAI ART AUCTION in yellow Chinese characters pinned to red in the manner of the old propaganda slogans. Floral arrangements of red gladiolus, white lilies, and shiny pink artist's palettes burst from the window bays like fireworks. The giant chandelier overhead quivered in the warm air as the crowd below fanned their catalogs. Those milling at the back craned their necks to see.

The veteran auctioneer had florid cheeks and a red polka-dot bow tie. He stood on the podium and performed like a stand-up comedian. As one lot number followed another, offered to the audience by a revolving trio of young women in body-hugging cheongsam, he kept up his excited patter. He had been brought out of retirement for the occasion, but his skills had not gone rusty. He had worked part-time as a tour bus guide for as long as auctions had been banned in Shanghai, keeping his patter up to date. The Communist Party condemned auctions as decadent, but how people loved them, the flowers and the lights and the gorgeous girls, so grand, so theatrical! And now auctions were back. The auctioneer mopped his brow as if the heat was too much for him. Bidding was brisk, bouncing from left to right and front to back. The atmosphere bubbled.

Shen, watching from the wings, had butterflies in his stomach. He wished Ricky was going on, rather than himself, when the auctioneer took a break. But Ricky was busy on the floor spotting bids, signaling the sharp-eyed veteran who would conjure a rival bid from the opposite corner before anyone had time to check.

Lot 39! Dehua-ware Guanyin, Ming dynasty, with the mark of He Chaozhong the maker on the base. One of the starlets, in beaded purple velvet, held up the figure of the Goddess of Compassion. Perhaps someone in the audience coveted the girl more than the Ming goddess. By buying the sinuous pearly-white porcelain for a punishing price the lucky bidder could also buy mercy on his voracious desire. The porcelain bodhisattva turned in her white-gloved hands. The flushed auctioneer fished for bids. The members of the audience held their breath and waited.

Shen observed the crowd from the wings, searching for a sympathetic face, but everyone was fixated by the precious object paraded up front. Then he glimpsed a young woman, with light-colored hair, at the rear of the ballroom. Her face was different. He wondered what she was doing there. Then she was hidden from his gaze by the jostling bodies.

Bids jumped in ten-thousand-dollar intervals, then five thousand, then one, until it came to a duel between an angular gray-haired woman from a German museum, who consulted her colleague before each increment, and a portly, pock-marked, poker-faced Chinese gentleman in a black suit and club tie who was known as one of Hong Kong's vainest collectors. He was plugging away in thousand-dollar steps to which the German museum representative responded after longer and longer deliberations each time. Finally, when she understood that her opponent would never give up, he got the prize. He stood to take a bow, acknowledging the applause from the floor without a flicker of emotion. Winning for him was a matter of face. A new record had been set.

The auctioneer, still mopping his brow, left the stage in triumph escorted by the three beauties who shuffled along behind him in their tight gowns, clapping their hands rhythmically like a trio of soft-shoe mermaids.

In the wings the veteran shook young Shen's hand for luck. He was a hard act to follow and Shen was nervous.

"It's a great opportunity for you," Stanley said, slapping Shen on the back as he pushed him out onstage.

The young woman at the rear of the crowd positioned herself where she could see the whole scene. She was a Caucasian, a foreigner, with wispy fair hair cut short around her face. Her plucked eyebrows made two little floating half moons above her big eyes as she folded her arms across her chest and enjoyed the spectacle. Since no one stopped her, she had just followed her nose, floating in the main door by the sign on the street, weightlessly ascending the grand winding staircase, trailing her hand along the iron rail that was polished smooth by countless hands. The funny auctioneer's hair was dyed black, she noticed, gazing across the packed ballroom. She was attracted to noticing such details. She liked looking at things. And now a different auctioneer was stepping forward, a younger man, approaching the podium in a gingerly manner.

The next lot was a scroll painting by Zhang Daqian, the prolific old artist, ex-forger, world-traveler, sham, who ended his life in Taiwan. The artist's chop was authentic, Shen knew, making the work reliably something from the studio if not from the artist's own hand. But Shen had little enthusiasm for the splashed ink painting of blurry abstract landscape in the artist's signature kingfisher blue. The bidding, as it commenced, was respectable, driven by Taiwanese interests who were patriotically concerned to maintain the value of their national treasure. Shen's eyebrows flickered as he struck the gavel with excessive force to declare the piece gone. Glancing across the heads in front of him, as people shifted in their seats before the next lot, he caught sight again of the fair-haired young woman at the back. She seemed to be staring at him quite candidly. Her face, encouraging him, was like a glowing apple, cheerful and unexpected.

Shyly he looked down at the order of proceedings and announced Lot 41. The model in burgundy studded with diamantés carried the object invitingly. It was the book.

Shen recognized its red cloth covers and familiar silk ties. He had forgotten where the book came in the order that he had arranged. In front of him was the crowd, hungry to be fed, but suddenly he could not bear to offer the book up to them. An old edition, an incomplete book at that, it would yield a trifle compared to the porcelains, the paintings, the precious jades that thrilled the audience with the prospect of high prices. And Shen wanted only to finish reading it himself, to experience what the author, Shen Fu, had to say before letting the book go on its way through the world. As the girl drew near, he saw that the book was upside down in her white gloves. He was shaking. For Old Weng's sake he was committed to achieving a good price. The old man had not parted lightly with his precious things. But no one really cared about the contents of the book. What if it failed to make the reserve, there in the grand ballroom under the bright lights, with a novice auctioneer calling the bids? It would be a dereliction of his duty as a connoisseur, a humiliating failure.

On an impulse Shen reached out and took the book from the girl's hands.

"Our deepest apologies, ladies and gentlemen," he announced, hiding the book under the podium, "Lot 41 has been withdrawn from sale. We sincerely regret any inconvenience. We move on now to Lot 42."

Shen herded the startled starlet off the stage by waving his hands at her as if she were a sheep. The crowd fluttered their catalogs at this glitch in the proceedings and tittered. Ricky rolled his eyes at Shen across the room and Linda, sitting at the side of the stage, frowned for all to see. Stanley gauged the extent of what had gone wrong by Linda's expression of disapproval and buried his head in his hands. The Deputy Mayor's private secretary was sitting right there in the front row with Ivy. Stanley wished the man had not shown up after all. He should not have entrusted such an important job to Shen. He could have hired another veteran, except that Linda had told him not to waste the money.

"Lot 42, the pièce de résistance," announced Shen, "the Qianlong oxblood bowl." That hushed the room instantly and the oncoming model was all at once made aware of the power she held in her hands. Her fingertips waggled. Her gloves did not fit. She was frightened of dropping the bowl, panting as she stood before the crowd, balancing the piece on her open palm before the eyes of the whole room.

"For twenty thousand dollars," Shen began modestly.

From there it was a race, as if a flock of homing pigeons had been released. He could not see where all the bids were coming from.

"Over here!" called Ricky.

The German museum woman again. The Hong Kong collector. An old tycoon's wife from Singapore. A limber sort of American fellow buying for an institution in California.

The fair-haired young woman stared so intently when Shen's eyes flashed past her that he almost signaled a bid from her.

One-hundred-and-twenty-four thousand dollars . . . a nod from the front row and no one would go past it. A tiger had roared. A second record was broken. People cheered as if some of the good fortune might brush off on them.

Utterly relieved, Shen gave a halfhearted bow to the audience and, hoping no one would notice, tucked the book under his arm and walked off the stage.

"Well done, kid," said Stanley, rushing to intercept him. "That little bowl will go down in history. What was the screw-up with Lot 41?"

"I meant to pull it before, Stanley. I'm sorry. I've been so busy. You know these old Chinese books–they take time. The title is wrong. *Six Chapters of a Floating Life*. It's not what it says it is. There are only four chapters. Four separate little booklets. Not six. If we sold it in this state, the buyer would only demand a refund. I'll go back to Old Weng and see if he's got the rest of the book. We can put it in the next time around."

"Linda says it made us look like bumpkins in front of the Deputy Mayor's representative."

"Don't worry, Stanley," beamed Shen.

"It was an awkward moment," said Stanley. But again from the room came applause, like the sound of a wave breaking.

"Listen to that, Stanley," said Shen. "We're there."

✷ ✷ Stanley shook hands with the dignitaries in the foyer. Linda stood by his side.

"Congratulations, Mr. Hummel," said Zhang Jun, the Deputy Mayor's private secretary. "What a memorable day! I was tempted to bid myself, but the prices you get are truly frightening. You've proved that we know how to run an auction here in Shanghai."

"It's a Shanghai tradition," Linda chipped in.

"What I wonder," Zhang continued, "is where you find such things. How can you be sure what they are?"

Zhang was in his forties, fit and virile, with bright oily eyes and an erect posture. He was an urbane, well-connected apparatchik. That made him untouchable as long as he was not too flagrant in his self-seeking. Having been schooled by the Party, he had the benefit of self-discipline. He tried to avoid body contact with Linda's niece even as she bent toward him. With her hair excessively curled, Ivy looked like a stuffed stocking in her fancy knitted outfit. She was charming but she had reached the age where, according to local wisdom, she was perilously close to being on the shelf.

"Oh, we have a brilliant young man working with us," Stanley burst out. "A true Chinese art expert who has come back from the States fully qualified and has taken to this business like a duck to water. You saw him up on stage."

"The young guy?" asked Zhang.

"You are correct," said Stanley. "You probably know his father. The history professor at Fudan University."

"Where is Sean?" asked Linda impatiently. "Sean!" she called in a voice loud enough to be heard backstage.

Shen was packing objects for their return to the office safe. Not many buyers had cash in hand to take home their prizes on the day. Only me, he thought, nervous of the book in his bag. He put it out of sight as he went to answer Linda's summons. He must explain to Old Weng as soon as possible.

"You know my niece Ivy," said Linda as Shen approached.

Ivy blushed and looked into the distance. Zhang stepped forward and shook Shen's hand. "So you're the expert. A pleasure to know you." He looked the young man up and down, appraising him in an instant, then turned and walked away, leaving Ivy not knowing whether to follow him or to stay talking with Shen.

"Excuse me," said Shen with an awkward nod. "I have work to do."

Ricky was sitting at the service desk behind a pile of catalogs as the crowd headed for the door. The fair-haired young woman threaded her way toward him.

"Hi," he said with friendly bluntness. "You want one of these?" He passed her a catalog. "No charge."

"Can you do me a favor?" she asked. Ricky noticed her Australian accent. "I'm having a show of my own work. I've got some invitations here. Would you mind if I left a few on the table? These people have got so much money. Maybe if they missed out on their heart's desire, they can buy one of mine instead."

Ricky laughed. "You're too late. They're all going home."

"Thanks," she said, passing him a bundle. "You never know who might show up."

"Ruth Garrett. Contemporary Traditional Chinese Painting," Ricky read. His brow furrowed. "Cool." He put the pile of invitations in front of the leftover catalogs. "Let's see who we can hook."

She gave him an embarrassed smile. She was grateful. But vague and disconnected, Ricky thought. She came across as the sort of person to whom things just happen.

"Maybe I'll come along myself if that's all right," Ricky said.

"Excellent."

"All right if I bring a friend?"

"Sure," she said, drifting away already.

"Here," said Ricky, flicking Shen the invitation when they had finished loading the catalogs and auction items into the van.

"Got a cigarette?" Shen asked. "You know I hate contemporary art."

They leaned against the cream-colored company van as they smoked the Yunnan cigarettes. Above them the new hotel towered into the mountains of shining clouds.

"You did brilliantly," said Ricky. "But I preferred the old man. He was good value. Can you believe those prices? There's money to burn in this town. Hey, what was that business about the book? That's the same book you've been reading, isn't it?"

Shen nodded. *"Six Chapters of a Floating Life."*

"That's the one. What happened? Was there something wrong with it?"

"No, but I haven't finished reading it yet."

Ricky snorted. "You wanker. What did Stanley say?"

"I couldn't just throw it away like that," Shen explained, still in some surprise at his own behavior. "I told Stanley it was because the book was missing the last two chapters. But that's the whole point. The ending of the story has been missing since the time it was first discovered."

"Yet people go on reading it?"

"I guess some people don't worry too much."

"Maybe there never was an ending," suggested Ricky. "Maybe the author just gave up."

"But it's the story of his life," insisted Shen. "That must have an end."

✷ ✷ The oxblood bowl had been bought by a young real estate developer who was well on the way to his first *yuan* billion. He was engaged to be married and wanted his bridal home, now under construction, to be appointed in traditional Chinese culture. His agent bid for him at the auction, but he came in person with his fiancée to collect the bowl. She kept poking his midriff through the training suit he wore, black with white stripes down the arms and legs, making the fabric crackle.

"I won't lose on it," he said, parking his sunglasses on his head and holding the bowl up, "that's for sure. There's not enough of the real stuff to go around for when all us Chinese are millionaires. Here you are, treasure." He passed the bowl to his fiancée and pulled his shades back down.

Shen took the bowl from her hands and wrapped it in several layers of bubble plastic.

"Thanks, buddy," the man said, slinging an arm around his fiancée as he swaggered out.

Shen's aesthetic snobbery came to the surface when he was rubbed the wrong way. He was pained that it had to be like this, that those with money were more likely to despoil the culture of the past than save it. To console himself he went back to his desk and took out *Six Chapters* and continued reading from where he had left off. The dictionary that he needed to consult for some of the classical words was open in front of him.

I remember that when I was a child, I could stare at the sun with wide-open eyes. I could see the tiniest objects and loved to observe the fine grains and patterns of small things, from which I derived a romantic, unworldly pleasure. When mosquitoes were humming around in summer, I transformed them in my imagination into a company of storks dancing in the air. When I regarded them that way, they were real storks to me, flying by the hundreds and thousands, and I would look up at them until my neck was stiff. Again, I kept a few mosquitoes inside a white curtain and blew a puff of smoke around them, so that to me they became a company of white storks flying among the blue clouds, and their humming was to me the song of storks singing in high heaven, which delighted me intensely.

"I'm dragging you away, old son," said Ricky, coming up from behind him. "We've got an art opening to go to and cross-town traffic to contend with. Something contemporary for a change. You spend too much time with things of the past."

"I'll bring the book with me," Shen decided. "What's the point locking it up in the safe all night?"

Shen stood up, put on his jacket, smoothed the lapels, and checked the knot of his tie in the window. A dove-gray haze had settled over the city. Away in the distance, beyond the river, the sun was melting like a scoop of watermelon ice cream. Ricky watched Shen tidy his hair with his fingers. Then Shen turned and smiled, ready to go.

Taxis, private cars, motorbikes, bicycles, buses full to the gills, trucks pushing into the fancy shopping area where pedestrians swarmed–the downtown streets were jammed at this time of day. So many boutiques and luxury department stores, so many street stalls and little bars and noodle shops, so many people on their way home or already on their way out again for the evening, making an avid audience for displays of style, all along the road where Ricky and Shen's van crept at a snail's pace.

Ricky let the van lurch forward as two long-legged young women strode out in front of the traffic without a second glance, like cranes crossing a field.

"Nearly got them," he laughed.

One of the women turned and swore at him in her roughest Shanghainese, so everyone could hear. Bystanders pointed at the foreigner with sneering laughter. Ricky could do nothing but honk his horn in a feeble riposte. Shen was unimpressed. He looked down, losing himself in the page of the book that was open in front of him.

✱ ✱ The gallery was a pristine room on the fourth floor of an office tower. The pictures hung on wires from a ceiling track, bathed in white light. A gaggle of Chinese and foreign artists, investors, and models floated through the space in an ornate pattern followed by a solitary waiter with a tray of champagne flutes who made a pattern of his own. Ricky wanted to chat, but Shen's intention was to look at the paintings first, so they separated at the entrance. Shen found himself wondering what he was doing there.

The pictures were all the same size, no bigger than a book, each identically mounted as a vertical scroll in a carefully selected range of colors. They were painted with precision and intensity in the traditional style known as exquisite brush. It was unusual to see it done so well. Shen found it hard to believe that a foreign woman could achieve such skill in this virtuoso style. Exquisite brush painting not only drew attention to the details of the subject the artist painted–flowers and birds, occasional other creatures, rarely people–it also drew attention to the artist's illusionistic expertise. It was a painstaking, rarefied way to paint.

In each picture there was a contrast between a traditional element and something contemporary. A black-and-orange butterfly alighting on a computer screen. A densely petaled pink peony blooming on a windowsill that overlooked a demolition site. A crane (the bird) flying past a crane (the machine). A tiny gold Buddha sitting beside an ultrasound scanner that showed the shadowy form of an unborn child. The past and the present juxtaposed. Creation and destruction. Nature and technology. Contending powers. Yin and yang. Each picture was stamped with a red seal.

Shen realized he was reading the pictures for signs that showed the artist to be an outsider to Chinese tradition. Or a certain clumsiness in the imagination or the composition that might equally indicate an insider trying to break out. He had completed a circuit of the gallery and had reached the first painting again–a dragonfly on the rotor blade of a helicopter–when he heard a woman's voice from the center of the room.

When I was a child, I loved to observe the patterns of small things, from which I derived a romantic, unworldly pleasure. When mosquitoes were humming around in summer, I transformed them in my imagination into a company of storks dancing in the air, which delighted me intensely.

He swung around at the words he heard and looked more closely at the speaker. He recognized her from the auction. He remembered her bright and staring apple face way back in the crowd. So she was the artist. Her gray dress was like a nun's habit. She had cropped hair and no makeup. She was talking to Luna Liu, who ran Shanghai's top modeling agency. In her black-and-silver suit and stiletto heels, Luna could not have been more of a contrast to the pale foreign woman. Luna had been a Red Guard commander in the Cultural Revolution. She could talk her way in anywhere. She never stopped generating business. Right now she was squeezing the arm of the artist–Ruth Garrett–as if she might eat her, or at least put her on the books at the modeling agency.

"Excuse me," said Shen, breaking in. He looked at the artist awkwardly, not knowing what to say.

"Are you going to buy a picture?" asked Luna, taking

advantage of the momentary silence.

"I don't have any money," said Shen with embarrassment.

"Do you have a card, at least?" Luna insisted.

"He does auctions," Ruth said.

"So you two know each other?"

"I've seen him at work," said Ruth, looking down.

Shen looked down too. That was when he noticed the embroidered Chinese-style shoes she was wearing. When he looked up, their eyes met. She had extraordinary green eyes.

"Where did you learn to paint like that?" he asked.

Luna didn't miss much. She was as aware of the intensity of the moment that passed between Ruth and Shen as if it had been happening to her. "Ruth was just telling me," she said. "When she was little she would see pictures in ordinary things, so that a swarm of mosquitoes could become like a hundred cranes to her imagination."

Then Ricky joined them, plucking a flute of champagne from the waiter's tray as he approached.

"Thank you for coming," said Ruth, "and for bringing your friend."

Luna looked from Ricky to Shen, then from Shen to Ruth trying to work out who was who. "There's a party on tonight," she said. "A celebration of your opening, darling." She patted Ruth's hand. "Have you forgotten that tonight is the night of the Cowherd and the Weaving Girl? Our Chinese Valentine. I'm sure you know all about that. I've hired the old temple garden at Jingshan and I've asked some interesting people. You're all invited!"

Shen scarcely heard Luna. Still echoing in his ears were the words Ruth had spoken earlier.

"What's the matter?" asked Ruth, waving her hand in front of Shen's face.

Shen looked at Ruth with new eyes. She had spoken the same words he had read that afternoon in the book. He was filled with questions and did not know where to begin.

"You haven't answered," she said. "Are you coming to the party?"

"Sure," he replied. "Thank you. Why don't we all go together? By the way, I'm Shen. Sean Shen. Like Sean Penn."

Ruth laughed. "But what's your real name?"

"My Chinese name is Shen Fuling." His eyes shone as he told her.

❋ ❋ The temple garden was water and rock, winding pathways and flights of stone steps overhung with willow fronds and brushed by shrubbery. The night was balmy and the mass of clouds across the sky was fringed by moonlight. Here and there in the magical landscape–wild and rambling in the impression it made, yet utterly contained and artificial–were red pavilions of different shapes and sizes, lit by paper lanterns, where people lounged on silk cushions drinking tea and wine or danced to pop music played on traditional instruments. The temple had been a favored spot for excursions in the tranquil old days before the foreigners came and Shanghai turned into a great trading port. So Shen told Ruth as they wandered away from the other guests. The original Ming garden had fallen into neglect long ago, but now the monks in charge welcomed the interest shown by businesswomen like Luna Liu and an effort at restoration was being made.

Shen asked Ruth her age. She told him she was twenty-four and had come to Shanghai from Sydney looking for a job. She had not found one, except for a bit of part-time English teaching to staff in one of the hotels. She spent most of her time working on her painting.

"Do you know about the Cowherd and the Weaving Girl?" he asked. "They are star constellations separated all the year round except for the seventh night of the seventh moon, when they are joined by a bridge. For one night only!"

People were drifting through the shadowy undulations of the garden, whispering, shouting, and laughing. The senior monk sat in an old rosewood chair grinning at all who passed. Through lattice windows an *erhu* melody wafted on the air. *Tie a Yellow Ribbon Round the Old Oak Tree*. Luna was dancing cheek to cheek with the tallest girl from the modeling agency. In her black-and-silver suit and snow-white dress shirt she looked like a panda dancing with a giraffe. On the other side of the ornamental lake, in the main pavilion, the waiters were arranging food, advancing and bending in the pink-and-yellow lantern light.

Shen knew the garden and its features. He had frequented it as a student. Ruth was happy to let him show her. They followed a winding path through a miniature bamboo forest and up a small hill to an open, six-sided pavilion just big enough for the two of them. It was screened from view on one side and overlooked the lake and rockery through angular branches of pine on the other.

"If only the moon would come out," said Ruth, looking at the restless sky, "then I'd be in heaven."

"It's close enough," said Shen with a tickle in his throat.

"I just want to get that little bit closer," said Ruth. She moved near him on the wooden seat and smiled. A stray tendril of the jasmine that was climbing up the pillars of the pavilion caught around her hair. She brushed it away, mistaking it for an insect.

Shen inhaled deeply. "The smell of your hair mixed with jasmine is wonderful," he said.

"Oh yes? I like jasmine."

"Its fragrance is too obvious," he retorted. "Too vulgar. Now there's a scent that's subtle," he said. Growing near the pavilion was a lemon tree in blossom. Shen put his head among its branches and breathed in. "That's the true gentleman. By comparison the jasmine is–like a nightclub entertainer."

Ruth came over to the lemon tree. Her dark dress and the warmth of her body brushed against him. "Then I suppose I'm better off with the lemon," she laughed.

Suddenly there was a plop in the water below. Ruth jumped, catching hold of Shen's arm. "What was that?"

"Was it a duck?" asked Shen.

They looked down where ripples crossed the lake, circle within circle to the far side.

"There's nothing there," said Ruth.

"There's a ghost in this garden," said Shen, lowering his

voice. "The temple is haunted. That's why people stopped coming here."

Ruth shuddered. "You're making it up. How do you know all these things?"

"A young monk drowned himself in this lake for love. He was tormented by the world of the senses. The other monks had wanted to drive him out. He was unable to detach himself from his desires. His ghost keeps returning to breathe the fragrant air of this world. He cannot let it go."

"Look," said Ruth, arching her neck. High in the sky the moon was coming out from behind the sea of silver clouds. "How beautiful," she sighed. The sky became a strange translucent blue. In the garden the line between shadow and light sharpened, giving an extra intensity to the jagged contours of rocks and bending boughs and a glittering sheen to the rippling water.

"So are you in heaven now?" asked Shen, delighted with Ruth's enthusiasm. Already her eyes had darted somewhere else. The changing pearly light and moving clouds exposed new beauties. In a niche in the whitewashed wall an orchid grew in a pot, its flower arching delicately outward. The moonlight cast a shadow on the white wall that was a little blurred, like ink wash.

"Oh, that is really special," said Ruth. "The shadow of an orchid cast by the moon is even more beautiful than the orchid itself, and if I could paint it, then it would be more beautiful still. To catch the accidental and fleeting, at one remove from the obvious thing–that's what appeals to me."

"I see you really understand beauty," Shen said.

Then a shout across the water broke their idyllic seclusion. "Hey," called a man's voice.

"Oh no," said Ruth. "It's Sun Da. He showed me around the city when I first arrived. I've been avoiding him."

Sun Da, with Ricky and a couple of other men and their girlfriends, lost no time in following the winding path to find Ruth and Shen. They tramped up the steps to the pavilion, laughing at having caught the couple out.

"So this is where you've been hiding!" Sun Da announced in Chinese. "I've been looking for you ever since I got here." He was a big man with a long black ponytail. He had tanned skin and sported long whiskers. He was an artist who worked in ink on paper, following the surges of his own energy, his *chi,* in wild, impulsive strokes. "Now that's a beautiful picture," he mocked, framing Shen and Ruth in the ornate pavilion with the illuminated landscape behind. "Who of you could paint that best?"

"There's something more beautiful," said Ruth firmly. "The shadow of this orchid on the wall. That's what we were just talking about. Who could paint *that?*"

"Maybe it's not necessary to paint it," said Shen, rubbing his chin. "Maybe it's enough just to see it and remember it when it's gone."

As if at his command, the clouds rolled over to cover the moon once more, the scene went dull, losing its sheen of moonlight, and the orchid's shadow disappeared. The others looked on, aware that something uncanny was occurring.

Ruth gave the faintest smile. She would carry the orchid's

shadow away in her mind.

Then Ricky broke the silence by swatting his neck. "Bloody mozzies," he said. "Don't you hate them?"

A gong sounded across the lake in three long resounding blows.

"Dinner is served," said Ricky, clasping his hands at his waist like a butler. "Better hurry before the vultures descend."

Agreeing with the Englishman's sentiment, Sun Da led his band back the way they had come, leaving Shen and Ruth behind.

Shen looked out over the scene for a last time to register it in his memory. Ruth revolved inside the pavilion, letting her arms float out as the moon bobbed its crest above the clouds again.

"You know what I really feel like eating?" she said, slowing her spinning. "A bowl of congee. I can't face the crowd in there."

Shen stared at her without quite knowing what he was seeing. He felt himself sinking, as if the ground were losing its solidity, turning to liquid beneath his feet, and he were spiraling through it at slow but gathering speed. He rocked forward on his toes, losing his balance, all the time gazing at her. It was as if a connection already existed between them, but where did it come from? She looked at him and he felt completely lost, but also found.

✷ ✷ They left the party and took a taxi back into the heart of the city, exhilarated at their escape. The driver dropped them at an intersection and from there Shen led the way down a side street to a place in the middle of a lane of food stalls that served the best congee in Shanghai. They sat on wooden stools at a rough table outside under the lights and ordered chicken congee with pickles and fried dough sticks.

"The moon's come out again for you," said Shen, looking up.

Ruth looked at him rather than the sky.

The bowls of rice gruel came steaming, the owner beaming at the pleasure the young couple would experience when they tasted the first mouthful. Ruth followed Shen's example by breaking the fried-dough sticks into the congee, then she added lots of pickled radish.

"Let's get some peanuts," she said. "Freshly roasted and heavily salted. And some smoked bean curd."

"You know what you like," Shen observed. "I mean–you like Chinese food."

"You don't have to be Chinese to eat Chinese food, you know. I like sour and salty things," she said, blowing on her spoon.

"You like congee?"

"I've always liked plain rice."

"The woman in the book I'm reading likes congee," he went on. "She eats it with her lover–with pickles and smoked bean curd."

Ruth shrugged. "That makes two of us," she said.

"What else do you like?"

"Ice cream," she laughed.

"I ate ice cream all the time when I was in the States," Shen said.

"Pity there's no good ice cream in Shanghai."

"I can show you where to find it. We Chinese invented ice cream."

"You people always say that," she responded. "The Italians invented ice cream."

"Your shoes," he said.

"I embroidered them myself. I know they're funny."

"I thought that only Chinese girls learned how to embroider like that."

"I went to a convent school where the nuns embroidered everything. My mother loved to embroider too. We used to do it together. That was how she got me to practice. Now it's just something I do." Ruth poked her feet out, curling her toes with pride. In the shadows the raised shape of the motif for double happiness was visible on each shoe. "I'm experimenting with Chinese colors and motifs," she said. "The nuns would be amazed."

Shen looked at Ruth's bare ankles. They captivated him even more than her shoes. "The woman in the book I'm reading is good at embroidery too," he said. "She embroiders her own shoes and they are the finest her lover has ever seen."

"What book is this?" asked Ruth.

"It's an old love story," Shen replied, "called *Six Chapters of a Floating Life.*"

"That's the book you withdrew from the auction. You

decided on the spot to withdraw it, didn't you? I wondered why."

"I wasn't finished reading it."

"Is that a good enough reason?"

"I've got it here," he said. "Can you read Chinese?" He pulled the book out of his bag and placed it on the table.

Ruth laid her hands on the book's red cloth cover. Then Shen undid the silk ribbons and found the passage.

When mosquitoes were humming around in summer, I transformed them in my imagination into a company of storks dancing in the air.

"Where does it say that?" she asked. "Are you trying to trick me?"

"Do you recognize those words?"

"Of course. They're my words."

"I heard you in the gallery, when you were talking to Luna Liu. The exact same words came out of your mouth. You were quoting from the book."

"How could I? I've never read the book. I've never even heard of it. Who wrote this book anyway?"

Shen turned back to the title page and pointed to the author's name. "He was a young man, a lover of beautiful things, the son of a humble official, who lived two hundred years ago. His name was Shen Fu."

"Shen," Ruth blinked. "The same family name as you." She looked again at the book, wondering if its pages could explain the connection she felt between herself and the young Chinese man seated opposite her.

2.

THE LITTLE PLEASURES OF LIFE

Shen lived in the old part of the city, in the attic of a rambling, run-down house that had been divided into a warren of separate apartments. Ruth was out of breath by the time they climbed the four flights of stairs to the top, and he unlocked the door and ushered her inside. It was dark, like a secret cave at the end of a winding ascent up a mountain path, and the floorboards creaked. He switched on the light and she saw the four-poster bed in the center of the room, carved rosewood with a floral quilt folded at its foot, the red lacquer screen with a table and two chairs in front of it, and a blue-and-white bowl filled with glowing oranges.

She looked around at the nest he had made for himself. The black roof tiles sat shipshape on the rafters. The window, covered with a honey-colored lattice, was open to the sky. There was a sink in one corner, and a gas ring and a row of cooking things. His Georgetown University baseball cap and framed class photo hung on the wall. An inflatable Ghostbuster dangled from a nail in one of the beams. He had a portable CD player, and a gilt Buddha with incense burned to ash on the shelf beside it. Things were as he had left them, his towel draped over the bed end; his weights on the floor; his tea mug, toothbrush and toothpaste beside the sink with an open packet of crackers; his laundry hung up on a line to dry.

"Do you like it?" Shen asked. "We used to own the whole house. My grandfather built it. Before I was born."

He put the kettle on the gas ring and while they waited for the water to boil, he told her the story.

Shen's grandfather had run the most modern printing press in Shanghai in the old days. He could not read at all when he started out, apprenticed to a typesetter as a child. The typesetter adopted him as his own son and he soon learned to recognize the shapes. In this way he developed an unerring attention to detail. Later he made his fortune producing advertising material in foreign languages. His credo was to do the job again for nothing if the client found a mistake.

Toward the end of his career he built the mansion of his dreams in the city's best neighborhood, a mock-Tudor pile of red brick, half-timbering and fancy stonework where he lived with his virtuous wife and a household full of devoted servants who had worked with him in the print shop when they were young.

His only sorrow was that his son, Shen's father, became a member of the Communist underground. But after the revolution the son's credentials with the Party stood the family in good stead. They managed to stay on in the grand house all through the 1950s. Only at the height of the Cultural Revolution was the house finally ransacked, and families of workers moved in. Again through the son's intercession–he was a cadre now–Shen's family retained use of the attic. Year in, year out, up four steep flights of stairs, they lugged the necessities of life. They even had to fetch their own water because the people below diverted the supply.

In that attic apartment, crammed with what remained of the family's fine furniture, Shen and his brother, Fuming, were born and reared. The grandfather and grandmother were bemused rather than bitter at the upheaval in their fortunes, but Shen's father came to despise the cramped, shabby space. Apart from being small and inconvenient, without modern facilities, it was a humiliating reminder of his family's unacceptable bourgeois background. At the earliest opportunity, when he was promoted to the faculty at Fudan University as part of the reforms that came after 1978, he moved into campus housing and sent his sons to the elite school there. Shen's mother went along without complaining. She was glad not to have to walk up anymore.

The attic was locked up for years and the dormer window became encrusted with swallows' nests. It stayed that way until young Shen came back from the States. By this stage, private ownership was acceptable once again and the family could have put up a case to regain control of the whole house. But for some reason Professor Shen was reluctant to do so. A case like that cost money, he said, and could drag on for years with no guarantee of victory. His wife was having trouble with her eyesight, he added, as a kind of excuse. Instead he granted Shen permission to live in the attic temporarily.

"I furnished it myself," Shen said, "with what survived of the family property and a few pieces I picked up in the flea market. I've created my own poor version of the traditional scholar's studio."

"It's magic," she said.

He lit a candle, turned out the light and moved the bowl of oranges over. Then, unlocking a glass cabinet, he took out two small porcelain cups. They were like miniature goblets. He poured out the steaming green-gold liquid and gestured with an open hand for her to take one.

"Have some tea," he said, picking up the other of the pair and holding it up to her with both his hands.

"They're beautiful," she said. The bowl fitted her palm snugly, warm and smooth as an egg. The exterior was decorated with tangled vine leaves and rouge-red grapes. Inside was a blue reign mark, over which a tea leaf floated like a ragged cloud.

"They're Ming dynasty," he replied. "From the court of the Chenghua Emperor. A perfect pair of *doucai* stem-cups."

"And you still drink out of them?" Ruth said. "I like that."

"It's the first time," he said. "Cheers!" Then he took a sip.

His lips–pink and half-open–revealed his teeth. He set

down the cup carefully and rubbed his eyes. He seemed to be in a kind of dream, as if he were losing some of his own definition.

Ruth surprised herself by wanting to reach out and touch him. She moved to the edge of the bed, and Shen came and sat beside her. They looked through the window at the moon coming out from behind the clouds. The bright moonlight cast the lattice's shadow, like a cage, over the floorboards.

"Everywhere on a night like this people are staying up late and looking at the moon," he said.

"But when there are two people looking at the moon together," she replied, "they can only be lovers."

"I don't think there is another couple like us looking at the moon," he said, hinting that they were not lovers yet.

"The moon makes people lovers," Ruth said.

"Even if they don't know that they are?" wondered Shen.

"What are you saying? Is that something else from the book?"

"No, but like the Cowherd and the Weaving Girl, some lovers only come together when the movement of the celestial bodies allows."

"Where's the book?" she asked. "Show me."

He brought the book over and they settled it across their knees, open at Chapter One. Shen pointed at a Chinese character with his finger and pronounced it, word by word; together they attempted a rough translation into English. As she got the hang of it, Ruth would freely interpret the meaning according to her own imagination. In this manner they worked through the text, acquainting themselves with Shen Fu and his charming, idiosyncratic bride, Yun, their friends, helpers and kin, and the joy they made with no one but themselves, discovering the beauty in things, living by no rules but their own.

The candle burned down and Shen lit another. Another hour passed, and the second candle burned out. They drank tea to stay awake, lying propped against pillows, half-snuggled under the quilt. The moon-shadow of the lattice over the window stretched across the bed and over their bodies. The scents of jasmine and lemon, the faintest traces from the temple garden, lingered in the air.

They read on through the sequence of old black characters, the progression of columns, the string of pages, weaving themselves between the lines as they followed the current of words, thoughts, and feelings. Sometimes, facing the page, was a woodblock image. A vase, a screen, a weirdly shaped rock. Two women. A boat on the water. Sometimes the meaning wouldn't come and Shen reached for the Chinese dictionary, the mighty three-volume *Ocean of Words,* to check a character. More often from looking at the parts of characters and associating meaning with sound they could guess what was intended. Their translation was more like shorthand, revealing the experience captured within the words, which they felt in their own flesh and blood.

"*Yun?*" Ruth asked. "What does her name mean?"

"It's a kind of herb, a fragrance, slightly bitter, like healing medicine."

"What would that be in English?" she wondered, insisting that Shen look it up in the Chinese-English dictionary.

The print was so small they could hardly see it. Shen pointed at the spot with the long nail of his little finger and Ruth peered with her eyes.

"Rue," she said.

"Ruth?" he asked.

She prodded him with her elbow. "*Rue,*" she repeated, louder, catching at the words that flitted through her mind. "Rue, the herb of grace."

"What's that?" he asked.

"Something I learned in school." She pushed away the dictionary and snuggled closer to him. They pulled the quilt right up to their chins, nestling together in the chill that was coming with the dawn, until they were so sleepy that they could read no more.

The timbers of the temple pavilion gleamed in the candlelight as if they were red wax and would melt in the warm dim glow. A forest of incense sticks grew from ash in a bronze brazier, filling the air with fragrant smoke that made eyes water and shine. The bride sat on her rosewood chair under a red veil. Her knees, sheathed in red velvet, knocked together like apples on a wind-shaken bough. She steadied herself by pressing her embroidered shoes flat against the floor. She had embroidered the shoes herself for the occasion. Beside her on a matching chair sat the groom in a charcoal gown with a red rosette at his shoulder. All she could see of him were his long pale hands resting on his knees like two shells. She knew he was trembling, like a wave of the sea at the point of breaking, holding the moment when the tide turns and the water surges in a new direction.

The distinguished guests were making speeches. Madam Liu, the opulent go-between, had spiked her hair with pearls on golden pins. The groom's honorable father, Old Shen the scholar-official, furrowed his face and screwed up his eyes in the stern expression of an ancestral portrait. A woman who looked wise stood at the bride's side with a sleek professional man. Weng, octogenarian Daoist, was there in tattered vestments, as was Sun Da, literati painter with ruddy cheeks and flourishing whiskers, his hair flowing in the manner of a knight-errant.

The head monk struck a gong and began intoning the words. He was as lean and pliant as a stick of bamboo. The wine was ready on the table in front of the groom with a pair of cups set out. The groom's face was on fire. He trembled with passion for his bride who sat beside him, hidden from his sight.

The monk bowed. He poured out the wine, filling the cups brim full. He had a birthmark on his left cheek that looked like one half of the character for *gate*. The groom took the first cup. The surface swelled but not a drop was spilled. The monk guided the bride's hand to the second cup. She could not help spilling a dribble of wine as she raised the cup, allowing the groom to link his arm around hers and offer his cup to her lips under the red veil, while he lapped the spilling wine from her cup, feeling it burn as it coursed down his throat. In this way they drained both cups, tilting them with their hands as gently as a mother would when feeding a baby.

Sun Da came forward and bowed. He wished to present the couple with a scroll he had painted. The groom indicated that the painter should unroll his work and let everyone see it. Sun Da untied the bow and hung the scroll from a peg behind the altar table. Slowly he unfurled it. It was a painting of the Old Man of the Moon drawing a red thread between his fingers. Sun Da explained that it symbolized the passionate attachment of lovers in this life, and the assembled company clapped.

"I believe we will be together not only in this life but in the next life too," the groom whispered to his bride so no one else could hear.

"We will experience in the next life all the joys we are unable to experience in this life," Yun replied from under the veil.

"Man and wife in this life, man and wife in the next," murmured Shen Fu with satisfaction.

"Only in the next life," giggled Yun, "I'll be the man and you'll be the woman. That way we will experience things we have never experienced before."

The monk struck the gong three times with force and gestured to the young man that the ceremony was complete. Smiling in rapture Shen Fu lifted the veil from Yun's face. He bent forward and brushed her cheek with his lips so lightly that no one could see, so gently that she almost wondered if it was real.

✻ ✻ Ruth was asleep beside Shen in the bed. He did not want to wake her but as he touched his lips to her skin, she opened her eyes, hardly in surprise.

"I'm sorry," he blushed. "I dreamed . . ."

"Maybe we just continued the reading in our sleep," she said.

He pressed his lips together and pushed his tongue against his teeth, looking at her as if she were playing a trick on him.

A car was honking in the street. The morning-exercise music started blaring from the kindergarten down the road. Shen craned his neck out the window and saw a bulldozer heave into motion, clearing away the rubble of the flattened house next door. He shuddered, watching it.

He lit the gas and started ironing his shirt for work. "What are you going to do?" he asked.

Ruth felt her tufted hair and sweaty skin and went into the bathroom to wash. The kettle was puffing out little clouds of steam when she emerged. She looked around the room. Everything had been rich with shadowy color in the moonlight and candlelight, but in the morning the attic was bare and ghostly, like a faded photograph. She noticed the scroll painting that hung on the wall, and moved closer to scrutinize it. It was discolored from the smoke of generations and almost monochrome. The Old Man of the Moon was black against the browned paper, his eyes like raisins, his head lolling and grinning as he bent over his walking stick. From the thumb and fingers of the left hand to the thumb and fingers of the right wound a ribbon that under the smoky grime on the painting's surface was the color of an old bloodstain.

"It's the red thread," said Ruth.

"Did you dream that too?" laughed Shen.

"I can't have dreamed everything," she protested. "Some things must be part of myself." She looked at him teasingly.

"Where do you live?" he asked. "Is it far?"

"I'm renting a room in Xujiahui. I don't know how long I can stay there."

"Drink some tea."

He rinsed the two cups and poured fresh green tea. They sat on either side of the table raising the cups to their lips, already with a sense of repetition, of time moving in a circular pattern. They might have been drinking from the same stem-cups the bride and groom had drunk from in the book.

"How many times in one life do we make tea and drink tea?" Shen asked. "Pouring boiling water on a pinch of dried leaves. It's the commonest ceremony, isn't it?"

"You're full of such things," she said, amused. "I'm happy to meet you, Shen. I'm happy about last night. Thank you for everything."

"You can call me at work," he said. "The number's on the card."

"I don't have the card," Ruth said. "Luna Liu kept the card."

"I'll give you another one. Here. Let me write down the cell phone too."

"I'll be spending time at the gallery till the show ends. I desperately need to sell something. Can there never be art without money?" she sighed.

"That was the Communist dream." He stopped her as she rose to go, putting out his hand. "Ruth, I don't know what you feel about this. The two of us."

"It came to me in the shower," she replied. "We're like Paolo and Francesca in *The Divine Comedy*. Do you remember?

They start out reading the story of Lancelot and Guinevere one afternoon until they are so overcome by their own feelings that they can read no more. I learnt that at school too." She kissed Shen lightly on the lips. Then she was out the door, leaving the sound of her footsteps diminishing down four flights.

✸ ✸ Shen thought dreamily of Ruth as he hung in the crowded bus on the way to work. He thought of her paintings, her embroidered shoes, the ghost that had splashed in the pond in the old temple garden, the orchid in moon-shadow, their shared taste for congee. The sequence of moments had flowed with a compelling direction, and with each uncanny connection that arose between themselves and the book the sense of significance had grown. It was as if they were staring from the shore and glimpsing a shape, scarcely distinguishable from the motion of the sea, that in time would reveal itself.

Shen found himself wanting Ruth physically as he dreamed in the bus, as if he were already familiar with the sensation of being with her, as if his body knew her already. Then the bus braked suddenly and he clasped the rail to stop himself from falling. He thought of the red thread of passion wound tightly around the fingers of the Old Man of the Moon, the protector of couples. It was a cord that bound one heart to another, like one flow of blood through two bodies. Yet it was also a tie across space and time, as the wheel of life turned, bringing souls back to their bodies. It was a longing that never ceased until it found its object. It was the red thread of ever-renewing love. Was it possible?

His hair was combed, his tie neatly knotted, but still he was late for work. Ricky was quick to notice that his eyes were sleepy and he moved like a zombie. "What happened to you last night?" he laughed. "I thought you didn't like contemporary art! Stanley wants to see you."

Stanley liked to call people in for a chat over morning coffee. He liked to hear the gossip. It was his version of consultation. Although he was not supposed to smoke in the office, he usually lit up a cigarette during these sessions, stretching his leash a little when he was away from his wife.

Shen took the cigarette Stanley offered him and sank into the armchair. Stanley was wearing his best dark suit and French tie to celebrate the results of the auction, but his satisfaction was turning rapidly to anxiety about whether they could repeat the success. People in possession of good items had to be encouraged to sell. It was the old problem of supply and demand.

"Linda's coming in later on," Stanley said, exhaling the full-strength Virginia smoke. "She's bringing her niece along, and Ivy's bringing her friend Mr. Zhang."

"Zhang Jun?" Shen queried.

"That's him. The guy from the Deputy Mayor's office. He was so impressed with how we ran the auction that he's bringing in a pile of pictures for next time."

"Pictures, Stanley?"

"Scrolls," said the boss, trying to look inscrutable. "Good stuff from a private collection."

"Whose collection?" It was supposed to be Shen's job to

winkle things out of collectors.

Stanley ran a finger down his nose and settled it over his sealed lips. Then, since he was a talker and could not resist dropping bits of information that made him look good, he said, "Could be they come from the Deputy Mayor himself. We're not supposed to ask."

The corners of Shen's mouth turned up but he said nothing. He could see that over the years Shanghai's powerful politicians would have had plenty of opportunities to amass artworks and antiques by means that would not always bear scrutiny. Gifts. Bribes. Confiscations. Proletarian reappropriation.

"Mr. Zhang has agreed to let us assess the pieces. That means you, Sean. You're the expert."

Shen avoided Stanley's gaze. "I"m not a real expert, Stanley."

"You have only to put a value on them," Stanley said bluntly, scratching his ear. "An estimate of what they might fetch at auction. Enough to encourage him to let us have them. It would be a great expression of confidence in the company, Sean."

"The valuations are the hardest part of all," said Shen, rubbing his sleep-filled eyes. He anticipated trouble. He wished he had an excuse not to do the job, although he was curious to see the collection. You never knew when something wonderful would turn up. But he hated being pinned down and found himself thinking of Ruth, and, with an irresistible pull, the possibility of escaping from this venal world with her.

Linda swept in wearing a tailored suit with big brass buttons, the skirt revealing her thighs. Her makeup was like war paint. Ivy followed in her wake. Linda scolded Stanley for smoking and turned up the ventilation to get rid of the smell. She told Ivy to check that the mugs for tea were clean and the water already boiling.

Then Zhang Jun strode into Stanley's office and with an outstretched arm briskly indicated where his assistant could deposit the scrolls. One rolled across the low table and fell onto the floor. Ivy dropped to her knees and picked it up, smiling keenly as the assistant stepped forward to take it from her.

For some minutes they sat in a circle drinking tea. Following Zhang's example, the men lit up cigarettes.

"I like your office furnishings, Mr. Hummel," Zhang said. Glass surfaces, custom-made cabinets, synthetic purple upholstery on the spongy chairs, reproduction Tang figurines.

"We used a local interior design firm," Linda volunteered.

Zhang looked at his watch. "Well, let's get started," he said. "The collector I represent intends to rationalize his collection. He is willing to liquidate some pieces that no longer interest him. We have brought a preliminary selection for you to look at."

With that introduction the first scroll was revealed. They gathered round admiringly. Three boats were floating down the mighty gorges of the Yangtze River beneath a huge red-lollipop sun. The painting was inscribed with a poem, a date, a signature, and a seal.

"It's a striking piece," said Stanley.

"It has revolutionary spirit," said Zhang. "Done by Master Liu Haisu in the 1960s. I don't claim to know much about art myself. It's up to you people to examine these pieces carefully."

He gave a curt signal that they were finished with this scroll and Ivy started to roll it up. He rolled out the next one himself, allowing even less time for an opinion of the work to form before he indicated to Linda that she could put it away and the next one came out.

Linda and Ivy were sighing and gushing. "Each is more exceptional than the one before," said Stanley, delivering a verdict.

"These paintings have not seen the light of day for a long time," added Zhang.

He was content to leave the whole pile on the table and get a considered opinion later. "Even from these few things you can see that it's a collection of Chinese paintings virtually without parallel, which will be reflected in the prices people can expect to pay for them." It was all done fast and huggermugger. "Well, it's over to you."

Stanley rubbed his hands. "It's up to you now, Sean."

Shen curled his fists into his eyes, wishing the pile of paintings would vanish. Just then Ricky popped his head around the door to say there was someone outside for him. He picked up the cheeky tone in Ricky's voice. "Excuse me," he said, moving toward the door.

"Just one moment, Sean," said Stanley, extending a bear-like arm across Shen's way. "When can we expect the assessments of these paintings to be done?"

"Well," Shen demurred, "I don't know. It will need some research. That takes time. I can't say exactly."

Stanley puffed his cheeks. "We can't afford to shilly-shally over this. If you drop everything and concentrate on this job, I suppose you could come up with something by the end of the week?"

Shen did his best to hide his irritation. "I can't say until I look thoroughly at the individual pieces," he said. "I'll do my best."

With that he left the room, taking a deep breath as he crossed between the desks in the outside office.

Ruth was waiting on the other side of the main glass door. He could see her, hovering restlessly. She looked like a boy in her blue jeans, blue denim jacket, and baseball cap. She had on dark glasses and a pack strapped to her shoulders. She turned as he came through the door. As the door closed again behind him, he felt they were being watched from inside the office.

"I tracked you down," she smiled, turning her cap around the wrong way. "I hope I'm not interrupting anything. I just wanted to see you."

"Do you want to come in?" he asked, not knowing what to do.

"Can you get away?" she replied. "We could go somewhere nice."

"Where do you mean?"

"Just away," she said.

Sometimes he thought of taking an afternoon off, but the office routine always seemed to close in around him. Ruth's suggestion opened up the possibility of a little defiant freedom. "I have to go and see Old Weng about his book sometime soon. He lives up the river."

"Let's go," she said. "It's a perfect day for an outing."

"Just like that?"

"Why not? We only need what's in my pack. We can get stuff along the way. I'll wait for you outside on the street," she said, pressing the Down button. "Don't be too long."

Her eyes were sparkling at him. The decision was made. He went back into Stanley's office and sat nonchalantly with his legs crossed as if nothing had happened. Curled in the opposite chair, Ivy pouted at him. Stanley was signing a receipt for the scrolls that the assistant had laid on his desk.

"But Mr. Zhang," protested Linda, "the restaurant is expecting us. A simple meal–it's on the way back to City Hall and won't take more than half an hour of your precious time."

Zhang shook his head. He was making a determined exit. Stanley followed him to the door.

Linda guessed he had another, more important appointment that he was too discreet to mention. She turned her attention to Shen. "Don't you think he was impressed, Sean? Professionalism and efficiency! We set a good example."

"His younger sister was my classmate," said Ivy. Her hopes in him were disappointed already. As a coded afterthought, she added, "His wife's been made the Deputy Manager of the new international airport."

Conscious of Ruth waiting outside, Shen scarcely heard what Ivy said.

"We can all have a good chat over lunch," said Linda cheerily. "A good old get-to-know-each-other. I've booked the Thirteenth Beauty."

"Oh no, Linda," said Shen, "you should have given me some advance warning." He wrung his hands with exaggerated regret. "I have an appointment already."

"You can be a bit late," said Linda. "That's no problem. Make them wait on you."

"I can't be late," he explained. "These relationships–with dealers–are very delicate things."

Ivy gave him a pleading look. Shen was conscious of overdoing it, but nothing worked with Linda unless it was laid on with a trowel. He knew that Ivy saw right through him. She had a sweet nature. "Next time," he said, smiling apologetically.

But Linda wasn't giving up. When Stanley returned, she insisted again. It was more difficult for Shen to maintain his story in front of the boss who knew his ways.

"There could be some serious consequences if I don't follow through on my commitment," Shen said opaquely, bundling the scrolls into his arms and carting them to his desk. "I'll get on with this as soon as I can."

"That job's your number one priority, son," Stanley called after him.

The words bounced into the air behind him like raindrops off an umbrella. Shen fetched his things, including Old Weng's edition of *Six Chapters,* and hurried out. As he went down in the elevator, he stretched up on tiptoes, light as air.

✻ ✻ The ferry chugged out into mid-river. Ruth and Shen leaned against the rail on the top deck eating ice cream cones and Shen put his arm round her to stop her from being blown over the side.

The water was like churning, milky coffee as they left the historic waterfront buildings behind. In pale, high blocks the city extended until it was lost in haze. Long, low cargo barges plied between navy boats and passenger craft on the wide water. Along the riverbank were the remains of old wharves and warehouses, the timbers splitting, the mortar crumbling between the red bricks. Yesterday's revolutionary slogans were faded to pink in the concrete embankment walls. A potted rose bloomed on the deck of a moored houseboat among billowing laundry. Seagulls scavenged washed-up waste in sluggish inlets along the shoreline. All along the river were factories, their smokestacks streaming, and fenced-off lots and constructions sites, until the reeds started to appear and ramparts of mud were raised to reclaim paddies where crops of rice and vegetables swayed, brilliant emerald. Ducks patrolled the banks.

Ruth noticed the papercuts stuck to the cabin window of a passing fishing boat. Fluttering and torn, they depicted red fish and flowers, omens of fruitful marriage. On the fishing boat's low, flat stern the boatman had devised a series of bamboo-and-plywood elevations, using the limited space to make little rooms where the family could sleep. The effect was compact and wonderful. Then a gust of wind plucked Shen's tie out from inside his jacket and blew it into her face. And hills began to be visible in the distance.

Shen breathed in and when he breathed out he felt for the first time that it was truly himself who did so, breathing his own life back into the world.

"What are you thinking?" she asked.

I am by nature fond of forming my own opinion, without regard to what others say. I value highly certain things that others look down upon and think nothing of what others prize very highly. So it is also with natural scenery, whose true appreciation must come from one's own heart or not at all.

"Is that Shen Fu speaking?"

"How did you guess?"

"I prefer to lose myself in a landscape," she said. "Zoom in on one particular thing and disappear. Like that little boat–" She pointed out a tiny rowing boat that was checking nets along the distant shore. A humped man with a cloth around his head was hauling against the wavelets whipped up by the wind. She could just pick out the red handles of the oars as he went from float to float.

Then the ferry swung around as the river curved, and the rower receded into the distance. There was a navigable channel marked by poles. Ruth coughed. She went white when she did so, coughing again two or three times. She pulled a wad of tissues from her pocket and coughed something up. Then she crumpled the tissues into a ball.

"Are you all right?" Shen asked.

"Those fading slogans remind me of my mother," she said. "She always read things wrongly, as if the words were vanishing before her eyes. She always worried so much about the future. That was her anxiety, after my father left, and I inherited it."

It might have been the salty wind from the ferry's wake that made Ruth's eyes water, but she screwed up her eyes because she did not want Shen to ask any more questions.

"You must miss her," he said quietly.

"Do you think it's fair to be punished for not knowing how things will turn out? That's what happened to my mother. She took the risk, anyway."

"What happened?" he asked. "What was the risk?"

Ruth's mother, Marie, was French, a convent girl like herself. She had gone out to New Caledonia from Paris as a committed young woman with the idea of making a new existence there. She fell in love with a local man, a Caldoche called Luc Garrett, who said his grandfather was an Australian merchant marine, and without thinking at all how it would turn out, she married him.

Her father was handsome, Ruth remembered, a popular man on the palm-fringed island shores where she spent her childhood. But even as a child, Ruth knew that the future was uncertain. Cloistered with the nuns, she never became attached to her surroundings, as if she knew her future did not lie there. When her father walked out on them, Ruth and her mother moved to Sydney. Ruth was fourteen at the time.

She was a student at art school four years later when her mother's illness was diagnosed. The doctors promised a positive outcome if Marie submitted to the treatment they prescribed. She was admitted to the best hospitals and followed the doctor's instructions with religious zeal, yet never with a very clear sense of what it was all about. In the end nothing worked. Giving vent to her anger and her sadness, Marie sank into her pain–as Ruth saw it–and the cancer killed her.

Luc Garrett had a sister who lived in Sydney, Ruth's only relative in that part of the world. The woman lived with her husband on the outskirts of the city and had a busy life of her own rearing kids and thoroughbred dogs. She offered to take Ruth in and give her a family life, but it was so far from the art school that Ruth decided not to go. She never believed it would work out. She stayed on by herself in the little terrace house where she had lived with her mother, managing the rent from the small sum of money she was left. She accepted the fact that she was completely on her own and slowly grew used to her independence.

At art school she sat alone at lunchtime on a bench inside the sandstone cloister that had been a jail in convict days. Sometimes she went outside to the street, where the surface was cracked by tree roots and roughly patched, and leaned against a wall in the sun while funky kids ploughed back and forth. At night you could buy drugs or sell sex there or just weep your heart out, and no one noticed.

She had studied Chinese at high school and kept it up in night classes as an art student. By that time she had also found an old man to teach her Chinese painting. When her own illness was first noticed, it was her old Chinese teacher who advised her to see a herbalist in Chinatown, as if it were the only sensible thing to do. Her mother's experience had given her a horror of doctors. Then she decided to do something more drastic and set out for Shanghai.

Ruth looked out over the rail in the gusting breezes. The story was far too complicated to tell Shen. He did not need to know.

"It's like me coming to Shanghai," she simply said. "For the first time ever, the future has stopped worrying me. I don't know why."

Her only precautionary measure had been to see the famous local medical specialist, Dr. Jiang, who charged her so much for the consultation that she did not go back.

She might have been a ghost in her own life before this, she realized. But now suddenly the present was enough. There was a destination that she did not question.

The little rowboat with the red oars had finally disappeared altogether, bobbing under the waves in the distance. Not loss, she reflected, only motion.

Shen found a place out of the wind and patted the spot for her to sit down next to him. They read some more of the book together, in the way they had done during the night, and they bit on melon seeds, scattering the husks overboard. She desired to touch him and have him touch her. But she did not say so. She only shifted closer to him on the seat.

One should try to show the small in the big, and the big in the small, and provide for the real in the unreal and for the unreal in the real. One reveals and conceals alternately, making it sometimes apparent and sometimes hidden.

✷ ✷ With a long blast of the horn the ferry approached the dock. Shen was familiar with the little canal town from an earlier visit to Old Weng. The streets leading away from the broad wharf were lined with restaurants and shops and old buildings that were poorly maintained. The old trees were so vigorously pruned that new growth shot straight from their thick trunks, and there were pots everywhere filled with brightly blooming flowers. Trade had brought culture to the town and, despite all the changes, there was a sense of beauty intertwined with its history. But the town's splendid past was little more than atmosphere now, an understanding that the town was thankfully out of the way of the present and could get on with its own business.

They crossed a bridge of white stone curved in the shape of a crescent moon. A path led along the bank of a canal where willow fronds hung in a curtain over the whitewashed walls of black-tiled houses. They reached Old Weng's house and Shen called from the gateway. The old man, dozing in a sunny corner, came out cheerfully. Shen's letter had arrived and he was expecting a visit. He nodded appreciatively, welcoming the young couple as his guests. His wife produced tea and small sweet bananas. The doors and windows were open and Ruth could hear the mewing of a cat outside on the wall. Old Weng had a pair of finches in a wicker cage hanging from the door beam. The cat came into view, a lithe tabby, eyeing the chirping birds.

Shen started to explain what had happened about the book. He felt obliged to justify himself. He should not have withdrawn the item from the auction without the collector's permission. He had simply not been able to control his desire for it, yet he did not have enough money to offer to pay for it. He did not know how much the old man would accept.

Old Weng still remembered Shen's face when he first examined the book, the expression of insatiable acquisitiveness that comes when you encounter something you have been seeking all along, unknown even to yourself, the thing that will allow you to grow, like a new bud on an old tree. Watching Shen on that occasion, Old Weng wondered if he had not deliberately passed the old book to the young man in order to see the enchantment work. Perhaps in that way he hoped to bind Shen to him by the wiry thread of connoisseur's longing that ties one generation to another, the past to the present. In any case, Shen should have the book.

"You can owe me the money. After a certain time if you are still unable to come up with the amount, then we will auction the book."

While they talked, Ruth looked at the things on display in the old couple's house. She was drawn to a round glass aquarium in which Old Weng's wife had created a tiny underwater world for their exotic fish. Weird little stones from Lake Tai made crags, caves, and towers around which the iridescent fish darted. Weeds grew from colored sand in the manner of trees bending over a pond. Fragments of china covered with green algae formed dwellings and bridges where tiny bamboo people gathered, their clothes fluttering as the fish swarmed around them like spirits.

The bowl that contained this little world stood on a square ebony stand that had been placed by the open doorway where the sun sparkled in the slowly moving water. Ruth knelt down to peer through the glass at the magnified scene. She remembered the miniature cork landscape her father had bought her in the general store in Nouméa one birthday. It was a fairy landscape from China.

The old man chuckled. "Your friend likes our scenery in a bowl," he said.

"She's an artist," Shen replied. "She loves miniature things."

"Just like Yun in the book."

Shen looked up, curious. He wondered if the old man understood. He was quick to believe that someone older and wiser might know how things fitted together. As with the most inexplicable of mysteries, we cannot believe that the understanding of them lies deep within ourselves and not in anyone else's experience.

"Where did you come by the book?" Shen asked.

Old Weng squeezed the tip of his long chin. "I had it as a young man," he said. "There was a street hawker in Shanghai who always had good things. He would spread his mat out in a lane near the Temple of the Old City God where all the dealers congregated, and one day when I happened to be passing, he called me over and said it was for me. The year was 1948, the same year Generalissimo Chiang spirited the imperial collection across to Taipei. What a year! There was so much stuff around and no one had any money to buy it, including me.

The collections of many lifetimes flooding onto the streets, liquidated for money that was worthless anyway. Cheaper than rice. Dirt cheap. I imagine the book came from the library of a gentleman from this region who was disbanding his collection before taking flight with the Nationalists to Taiwan. Maybe to pay for a son's passage out. Sending his inheritance out on the current.

"I nearly lost the book myself later. It's quite a decadent piece of writing, you know, if you have a mind to see it that way. I had it here in the house for ten years when I was under suspicion for my attachment to stinking old things. Well, I survived and it survived, and when I came looking for it after the chaos settled down, there it was, just as I left it, well camouflaged as part of Chairman Mao's works."

Shen was intoxicated by every detail the old man revealed concerning the book. He felt he had become the custodian not just of an object but of lives, history, and the miracle of continuity through the storms of time.

"The missing chapters," Shen stammered.

The old man nodded and sighed. "Ah yes! I hoped all the time that I would find them. Like every other bibliophile in the country. It was odds on that they would float to the surface in the chaos of those days. When I bought the copy from the street hawker in Shanghai, I gave him definite instructions about the missing two chapters. His network was vast and deep, back into the hinterland the length and breadth of the Yangtze River and all its feeders and tributaries. I did my research and ascertained that the author wrote the book under the Jiaqing Emperor but it did not come to light until it turned up in a secondhand bookshop in the reign of the Guangxu Emperor, the era of the Empress Dowager, already several decades after the author must have died. When I say it came to light, I mean only four chapters of the original six. Ever since then there has been much speculation about the missing chapters. A publisher claimed to have discovered them once, around the start of the anti-Japanese war when the Communists and Nationalists joined forces. It was an excellent literary forgery and made good money for its perpetrator. But eventually the hoax was exposed by a dedicated bookworm."

"What if they were never written?" suggested Shen.

"Oh, they were written. The man's life went on. Why *Six* if he only intended to write *four?*"

"Maybe something happened to him," said Ruth, joining in at this point. "Something that prevented him from going on."

"He would have written even that," countered Old Weng. "I stopped looking years ago. There is so much material missing everywhere. Where is completeness? If fate has taken over the authorship of the book, finishing it two chapters too soon, that is what we have, a chunk of the whole, a shadow of the actual thing, like all our knowledge and all our lives." He exclaimed with a laugh. "Too deep! Excuse me. A rambling old man. No, young Shen is right. Some day somewhere, misplaced among family papers in a dowry chest sold in a junk shop in Bolivia or New Zealand, fate the great author will give up those last two chapters. I have heard even now in Hangzhou there is a shifty dealer who claims to have them–"

Shen seized the arm of the chair and said, "I have to find them."

Just then the cat shifted its gaze from the birds to the aquarium, which just this once had been placed within its reach. The cat sprang from the top of the neighbor's wall and landed on the ebony stand. The bowl slid to the floor, as if in slow motion. Ruth's open hands framed the accident. She felt she could have stopped it, but the bowl smashed and she could not catch the water as it ran away, sweeping the tiny flapping fish across the tiled floor into the yard.

"Quick," she cried, bending down and cupping her hands to catch the fish while the water ran between her fingers. The cat bounded away in alarm, then slunk back and grabbed one of the fish.

The old man called his wife, who hurried in with a bucket of water into which Ruth dropped the fish she had caught. She chased away the cat and picked up as many of the other fish as she could find. But shamelessly the cat came back and ate one or two. Ruth picked the pieces of the little world from the mess of broken glass on the floor and set them on the stand, dribbling and forlorn.

"A whole world is shattered," she lamented with tears in her eyes. She felt responsible, for admiring it too much. "Even something so small gets destroyed," she said in shock. "I can't bear it."

"Even something so small brings out the jealousy of the gods," said Shen, putting his arm round her shoulder.

"Such is our life," said Old Weng, nodding.

✷ ✷ They wandered back through the streets of the town looking at funny things for sale until they heard the ferry's horn sound from the wharf. They ran and reached the dockside just as the boat was pulling out into the brown water. They threw their arms down helplessly and laughed. They had missed it on purpose–and now they had to find a place to stay for the night.

There was a drab hotel of several stories by the waterfront called the Golden Century, where business travelers and officials stayed. When they inquired for a room, the clerk at the reception desk asked to see their documents as evidence that they were married; because Ruth had no documents with her, he refused to give them a double room.

"I'm going to pretend I'm a man from now on," Ruth said angrily. "They wouldn't worry if we were two men wanting to share the same room, would they? But a Chinese man with a foreign woman and they panic. I was really looking forward to a hot bath," she complained.

"We can find a better place," Shen said. He didn't know how seriously to take her. "That place was not very hospitable anyway. We can find something else."

She laughed at his concerned expression. "It doesn't really matter."

They asked in the street and got directions to a small inn a little outside the town. Stone steps led up to the pair of closed double doors on which they knocked. When no one came, they knocked again. At last an old woman opened up. *"Wei! Wei!"* she called. She frowned at them, twisting her face and flaring her nostrils. Shen said that Old Weng had sent them and they wanted a room for the night. Without asking a single question, she whisked them inside.

The old woman showed them to a large room that looked onto a courtyard where bamboo luxuriated. Beyond was the canal. The bare room had a low bed for two and a washstand. Ruth spied a red peony in a pot in the courtyard and asked if they could bring it inside. The old woman grinned in response. She lived there alone except for one small grandson. Business was slow. She named a price for the room and Shen said they would have it if the price included meals. Meals were extra, she said. Shen agreed to her price if it included hot water for washing and if she would get them a bottle of the good local yellow wine.

The old woman, whose name was Mrs. Ma, said there was a bathhouse a few blocks away or she could boil up a big kettle of water on the stove and the young woman could wash in the tub in the courtyard. It was warm enough outside and no one would see her through the bamboo.

Ruth liked the idea. When two kettles of steaming water had been mixed with the cold in the wooden tub in the courtyard, she wrapped herself in her towel and stepped outside in the slip-on sandals Mrs. Ma had given her. Then she gingerly lowered herself into the water. If she made herself compact, she could soak up to her neck and ladle water over her hair. The breeze rustled the bamboo and when a boat passed on the canal, she could hear the voices in a medley with the lapping water. Mrs. Ma pattered to and fro with soap and more hot water, finding it all a great joke.

There was a baby pig running about in the courtyard with purple-and-black splotches on its pink skin. It poked and snuffled at the tub with its snout, making Ruth laugh. Mrs. Ma's grandson played peekaboo around the door, near hysterical at the strange girl with colorless hair and pale skin who ducked down below the side of the tub out of sight, then popped up and surprised him.

Shen sat inside smoking by the open window where he could hear Ruth splashing. She was hidden from his view by the bamboo, but he sat with his back to her in any case, content with the sound. He imagined her soaping herself on the neck and shoulders. Imagining his pleasure with her was part of the pleasure of desiring her, he realized. Pleasure lay in anticipation, in what was still just out of reach, not so different from the memory of past pleasure. He wanted her, and when she came in from the bath, her skin moist and fragrant, her hair wet, he felt the sensation of wanting her shoot right through him.

A smaller room opened off the bedroom where Ruth went to dress. "Shall we go out?" she called to him when she was ready.

"What about our yellow wine?"

"Let's have it when we come back. The day's still light. The wine can wait."

Mrs. Ma waved them off from the steps of the inn. When they returned, she chuckled, they would be hungry for the pleasure of her food and would appreciate its tasty simplicity all the more.

They walked up the hill following a stone road through

woods and terraces to the famous Buddhist temple of Tianzhou, the Yellow Corktree Temple. The air was cool and aromatic with just a whiff of night soil from the vegetable patches that were wedged into odd pockets of land. The road was busy with farmers and children, tractors, motorscooters, mule carts, as well as sightseers and monks from the temple. As they strolled higher the town below resolved into a quilt of black and pale gray bordered by shining strips of canal, and the ditches along the roadside became overgrown with melon vines and bamboo as the road climbed up and up between sturdy mud walls.

The Yellow Corktree Temple was named after a tree that once grew in its grounds. The temple's fortunes had risen and fallen since the patriarch founded it nine centuries ago. Its last period of prosperity was under the Ming. Since then it had hung on just this side of dereliction. The camphor trees and cypress pines were still standing, massive and stately, but the yellow corktree was gone. The ponds were slimy with weed, thick with fat fish. Under a brushing of pine needles the glaze of the roof tiles was worn. Ruth and Shen dawdled up the chipped stone steps, admiring the auspicious setting of the temple grounds, unchanged over time. They wandered from pavilion to pavilion beneath the old trees of the dusty gardens, and through back courtyards stacked with lumber for the continuing work of repair. Workers were sawing camphor wood for beams and the astringent powder swirled in the air. In one workshop an old man was pinching wet red clay in his fingers, showing the apprentices how to mold the warlike figure of a temple guardian three times his own size.

In the smaller hall was the statue of Guanyin, Goddess of Compassion, all dusky gold and serenity. She had radiated blessing there for many hundreds of years. She was draped from head to foot in a red-and-pink silk robe, a merciful mother who brought healing to the sick and offspring to childless women. So believed those who fervently lit their bunches of incense from the red candles blazing around the brazier outside the door. They blew out the flame and closed their eyes, bowing three times to this version of the bodhisattva, who had come originally as the male Avalokiteshvara and changed mysteriously on the journey through time into the female, all-loving Guanyin. Girls bowed to her in platform soles and gold dresses. Boys bowed to her in tweed jackets and trainers.

Then the monk who sat at the entrance of the main temple hall struck the gong. Its sound seemed to reverberate with the sun that was sinking in the sky and the gauzy golden light seemed to thicken. Crows cawed overhead, descending into the spiky pines. Parents called to their runaway children. Now the clapper sounded, the insistent knocking of wood on wood, and the low chanting of the sutras began, mumbled syllables that emptied the assembled monks' minds of all distraction.

Ruth and Shen found the pagoda at the back of the temple and, spiraling up its interior, climbed to the top. Ruth was panting, and Shen was out of breath too, as they surveyed the rose pink and orange of dusk smoldering across the plain that was threaded with waterways, shining in the distance like live wires. Their skin was warm against the soft old brick of the pagoda as they leaned from the balustrade. The rise and fall of their breath, the friction of clothing, and the touch of flesh against flesh soon aroused desire.

"Do you think anyone else feels like us?" Shen asked.

"I never felt this good. You're feeling it too, aren't you?" she replied, stroking him lightly between the ribs.

On their way down Shen insisted on finding a particular pond that was overlooked by an open shelter where a famous monk had sat for years in meditation. It was said that if you peered into the pond at sunset, it would reflect your image from a previous existence.

Carp, orange dappled with white, were cruising through the brown-green particles suspended in the water. Together they looked down over the broken stone railing. The setting sun flashed across the water in a blinding mirror of gold in which they could see themselves, for a moment gazing back as if through a fire of love, until the water rippled and the angle of light changed and the reflection broke up.

On the other side of the pond a burly man in a black leather jacket was peering for his reflection too.

"Ah!" he cried, reeling back.

"What can you see?" called his companions.

"A bloody monkey," he swore, and his friends laughed.

"What did you see?" Shen softly asked Ruth.

"The reflections overlap," she said by way of answer. "The woman's face and the man's are inseparable. The woman is me and not me."

The light of sunset blazed. The golden carp circled

beneath the water weed.

"She's Yun," he said.

"Then he's Shen Fu," she replied.

She leaned forward and put her hand in the water and the blurry reflection leaned toward her.

"You can't touch them," Shen warned. "The only way to reach them is by being them. That's what they want."

A fish leaped, gasped in the air, and dropped back with a splash.

Ruth was trying to figure it out. Then the reflection disappeared altogether as the sun sank behind the trees.

They walked through the last dark corridors of the temple, the old dormitories boarded up, awaiting the funds for restoration. Old Weng had told them about his friend, the head of the temple, a monk called Broken Gate, whose life's mission was to rebuild the Yellow Corktree Temple to its original state. Time was running out now for Broken Gate as well.

Ruth was still thinking about the reflections in the pond that were supposed to be reflections of another incarnation. "What you mean is that *they* have come back," she said.

"Not exactly," Shen replied. "*We've* come back. We've been given another chance." He put his arm around her to make the point.

"Do you believe that?" she asked. Her green eyes shone in the dusk like a cat's.

✷ ✷ Mrs. Ma set out bowls and cups on a square wooden table with saucers of spiced peanuts, fresh bean pods, and pickled ginger. There were dishes of fried eel, chicken, and frogs and greens that had a slight taste of mud. They ate ferociously and flooded their food with the yellow wine that Mrs. Ma had warmed. They knocked their feet together under the table and brushed arms as they ate, and clinked glasses until the bottle was drained and they were quite dizzy.

Then as quickly as the food came, the table was cleared and wiped down. Mrs. Ma told her grandson to lie down on his little mattress in the corner and be quiet. She said goodnight to them and turned out the light. Shen and Ruth stumbled to their room.

The glow that came from the open window gave a shadowy sheen to the peony on the windowsill. They did not even turn on the light to find their bearings but felt their way to the bed, floating, their heads spinning as they crawled into each other's arms and began to caress, moving their hands under their clothing, moving to touch skin.

They lay discovering each other, idly, excitedly, letting simple movements acquire the tantalizing power of repetition. Shen swirled the tip of his tongue inside Ruth's ear, tickling her, making her squirm and writhe. He traced all over her with his tongue, stimulating and relaxing her. Then she licked his smooth chest, around each hard flat nipple, making him moan and flex. He stroked the soles of her feet. His jaw muzzled her chin. Her hands clasped his sleek neck as they kissed deeply, she held him tight, and they held each other with their eyes, feeling the flow and braid of oneness.

Then Shen knelt between her open legs and she reached

for him, pulling him gently toward her. He lifted her close to him. He let her guide him until their bodies formed a circle, a tight ball. They yielded to the energy that flowed through the O of their bodies as if they were passing through a gateway of flesh to a dimension where the body of one incarnation joined with the body of another, as if the rhythm of their ecstatic love-making were the rhythm of time itself.

Shen experienced the sensation of entering the fire of another kind of existence. He had heard the expression *losing yourself in love,* of, at the moment of climax, forgetting who you actually are. He felt the same energy of binding and releasing, of one form dissolving and then coalescing in another. A reincarnation. A sense, a flash, a *smell* of intimations from those other lives. He made love and became another person who was also himself.

She stroked his face, covering his eyes with her hand. Then, as their passion subsided, the circle of their flesh returned once more to the horizontal line of two bodies asleep beside each other in one bed.

Mrs. Ma's grandson was spying through the keyhole even as the neighborhood roosters started to crow and the sun rose above the housetops. His grandmother smacked him, telling him not to wake the young couple with his naughtiness. "They've been at it all night," she said.

Then at nine-thirty Shen's cell phone rang with its insistent, unsubtle signal. He rolled over and groaned.

It was Ricky. Shen could hear the urgency in his sibilance. "Look, you better get in here fast, mate. Linda's on the warpath. They reckon the Deputy Mayor's about ready to take the bait and you've dropped the bundle. Get your skates on and get in here."

"I can't. I'm out of town," Shen answered sleepily. "I'm in Tianzhou seeing Old Weng."

"Then get from Tianzhou to bloody Shanghai by the fastest possible route if you want to keep your job. I'll tell them you called in sick and that you'll be here as soon as you can get on your feet."

"Thanks, Ricky."

"Ruth with you? You're a dark horse. Couldn't you wait till the weekend?"

"Thank you, Ricky. Bye."

Shen sat up and rubbed his eyes. "Oh God," he yawned. "We have to go back to Shanghai."

Ruth put on some clothes and went out into the sunny morning. A pair of sparrows was flitting in the bamboo thicket. She found a way through the bamboo to the wall. By standing on tiptoe, she could see over the top to the canal. A barge loaded with caged ducks was being poled along and a pair of ducks–a duck and a drake–were swimming rapidly in the opposite direction to escape into the reeds. Ruth rubbed her bare arms as, unobserved, she peered over the wall.

She wondered at the connection between this body of hers and the cycles of time, this body and the other multiple forms of existence that could be lived. She wondered where she and Shen could go now. She did not want to go anywhere else.

"Ha!" said the little boy, crashing through the bamboo to find her. He had a steamed bun in his hand, half-eaten, and was laughing at her.

"Can I have that?" she asked, laughing back.

He thrust it at her and she broke off a piece, which she tore into small crumbs and threw over the wall into the water. The male and female pair of ducks came to the base of the wall on the other side to eat. She could hear them quacking. "Listen," she said to the little boy, who didn't have his pants on. "Quack quack quack," she went.

Soon what was left of the steamed bun had all gone. She brushed her hands and held up her open palms to show the boy that there was nothing left. Not a single speck.

"Can we experience all things together?" Ruth asked agitatedly when she came in to find Shen. "Can we be all things to each other?"

"I don't know," he answered. "We can try."

愁

3.

SORROW

Our wedding took place on the twenty-second of the first moon in 1780. After the drinking of the customary twin cups between bride and groom, we sat down together at dinner and I secretly held her hand under the table. It was warm and small, and my heart was palpitating. I touched her breast in fun and felt that her heart was palpitating too.

"Why is your heart palpitating like that?" I whispered in her ear.

Yun looked at me with a smile and our souls were carried away in a mist of passion. That night when we went to bed, dawn came all too soon.

On the seventh night of the seventh moon of that same

year, Yun prepared incense, candles, and some melons and other fruits so that we might make offerings to the gods of the heart. I had carved two seals that we exchanged, with the inscription MAY WE BE UNITED FROM INCARNATION TO INCARNATION. That night the moon was shining beautifully and the ripples on the water were like silvery chains. We were wearing light silk clothes and sitting together with a small fan in our hands before the window. Looking up at the sky we saw the clouds sailing through the heavens, changing at every moment into myriad forms. Yun said, "This moon is common to the whole universe. I wonder if there is another pair of lovers quite as passionate as ourselves looking at the same moon tonight?"

"You dumb thing," said Linda ferociously. "Did you have a good time? Your boss asked you to do something and you just ignored him. You're too arrogant. Knowledge is nothing without the business side. Don't you understand that?"

Shen bowed his head and waited for the diatribe to pass. Then he said, "Why are you bawling me out, Linda, if Stanley's the boss?"

"You no-good thing. Stanley's too soft on you. Now get in there and prepare those assessments for Mr. Zhang."

Shen sat heavily at his desk. Ricky brought him a mug of coffee to cheer him up and left him to it without saying a word.

As Shen unfurled the first of the scrolls, his resentment sharpened. The brushwork was too even, too steady. The paper and the ink seemed to have faded at different rates.

Pulling books down from the shelf and peering with a magnifying glass, he was able to make comparisons with authenticated works. He opened the other scrolls and compared them closely. They were supposed to be the work of different masters divided by centuries, but there was resemblance in the materials and methods used. The seals, expertly carved in different styles, showed similar inking. He probed zealously, lifting away the layers that separated him from the truth.

He wrote a list of specific observations and stitched them together into an argument that all the paintings emanating from the Deputy Mayor's office were expert forgeries produced perhaps thirty years earlier as a virtuoso exercise in deception. Perhaps, Shen thought, they had been substituted for the real works in a collection that had been confiscated. Copies so good would not have been detected, while the real thing could be removed to a safe place.

He took ten deep breaths. He wanted to cool down before he presented his findings to Stanley. He must be careful not to implicate the Deputy Mayor directly.

Just at that moment he looked up and saw his father coming in through the glass door. Professor Shen had his briefcase in his hand and, unaware that his son was observing him, he entered the office with his typically worried, disapproving expression on his face.

He was a tall man with a broad frame. He had a good mane of white hair brushed stiffly back and an engineer's steel-rimmed glasses. He wore the same suit of fine-quality gray wool in all seasons.

"Dad!" said Shen, coming up and shaking his father's hand.

"I looked for you at the house last night," the old man said to explain his unannounced arrival. He glanced around the office, as if trying to place his son there. "You've got more computers here than we've got in my whole department," he said. It was a barbed remark designed to embarrass his son.

They sat in the corner by the window in the armchairs for guests and drank tea. Professor Shen was glad to have a bird's-eye view of Shanghai's development. From such a height the changes could be gauged with objective distance, the overpasses and tunnels and tall buildings, as if in a blueprint. From ground level it only looked like anarchy.

"So much investment," said the old man with satisfaction, wringing his hands as he steered the conversation where he wanted it to go. "If only we had some of that investment for ourselves, we would be in a growth situation. Capital is what it takes, I'm afraid. Your young brother's business is starving for want of a small injection of money. A golden opportunity has come his way. If you could help, son, the whole family would benefit. You know that he has the business skills–"

"Won't the bank lend him the money?" Shen asked. His brother had already squandered one loan.

"We must find another way," the old man replied. "That's why I've come to you."

Shen put his finger to his chest. "Me? I'm as poor as a mouse."

"You're in contact with money," said his father, his head

ducking left and right. "Shanghai Art Auctions International. You have contact with foreigners who might be looking for a promising little investment in Shanghai."

Shen shrugged his shoulders.

"If there is no foreign source to borrow the money from," the old man continued solemnly, "then we must rely on our own strength." With that he beat the palm of one hand with the closed fist of the other, his habit when quoting a revolutionary slogan.

"Strength?" queried Shen.

"Realize our assets."

"What assets?"

Professor Shen pulled an official document from his briefcase and spread it on the table. He pointed to the notification from the Shanghai Municipal Government stamped with red seals. "The municipality wants to demolish the old house."

Shen felt his cheeks burn. "They can't do it. Not just like that. It's impossible."

"It's inevitable," he said. "They'll pay compensation."

"It's the family house. It's your father's legacy to later generations. We nearly lost it once already. We must fight to save it."

"What use is it to us in its present form?" the old man retorted.

"Dad, I live there."

"You need a nice new apartment with proper plumbing. That's the situation, son. Think it over."

The indomitable old comrade rose to his feet. Shen saw

that the document on the table with all the weight of the municipal government behind it was nothing compared to the force of family obligation that his father was placing on him.

"Nice to see you. You're in good health. Take care," his father said. "I'll be going now."

"Good-bye Dad," Shen said limply, watching his father's gray-suited back go out through the gold-lettered glass door.

It was all wrong, Shen thought. The house had survived, one corner of it still in the family's possession, through decades of political upheaval. He loved that house. He loved the space he had created for himself there, his traditional scholar's studio. From that one corner he could rebuild the world as he believed it should be, reclaiming the house, room by room, floor by floor, as if the house itself was a force of renewal. The proof was there already in the dream he had shared with Ruth, the dream that brought Yun and Shen Fu back to life.

He returned to his desk and looked at his terse assessment of the scroll paintings. After the encounter with his father, he was not ready for another confrontation. He read over his own writing, the doubts raised clearly point by point, the larger inference building step by logical step.

He was also watching from the corner of his eye for Stanley to step out of his office.

When the moment came, Shen quickly slipped inside his boss's empty office and left the report lying in the center of Stanley's desk where it could not be missed. By the time Stanley found it, Shen would be out of the building and walking away down the street. Shen could imagine Linda's anger and

Stanley's suffering, but he had no choice. He had to expose the truth of the forgeries. The next morning he would arrive punctually at work and face the music. For now, however, he wanted only to keep the appointment he had made with Ruth when they parted that morning. Ruth would understand how he felt. She would support him. She would not disapprove.

✻ ✻ The gallery had sold three of Ruth's pictures. Apart from welcoming the money, Ruth was charmed to discover that there were strangers who appreciated her work. She was pleased to hear that two of the three buyers were Chinese. But she was tired and her head ached, and in this condition she could not concentrate. She went back to the room she rented to lie down.

A postcard had arrived from her father in New Caledonia. It was a response to the brief letter she had sent him with her address in Shanghai. He wrote that he had married again and had moved from town to a place on the coast where he was the manager of a new business. He did not say what. Her father lived his life by dealing with the opportunities that presented themselves. His daughter was not like that. She had a preponderance of imagination, making the life she lived never her only life.

One of her housemates, a young German banker, was at home and wanted to chat. He was always complaining about China and the Chinese. "You can never trust them," Wilfried exclaimed with wide-open eyes. "They lie. The Chinese lie." Ruth wondered what it was about Wilfried that made his experiences so negative. She was put off by him too, because he was unsympathetic toward other people's dreams. She knew, as she listened to him talk, that she did not want to stay on in that house. Even while she chatted she began stuffing clothes into her backpack. She told Wilfried they could give the room to someone else. She would be going away for a while. That was all she said. Then she went to meet Shen.

She was early so she hung about looking at the teeming fish in the ponds from different vantage points on the zigzagging bridge, keeping out of sight until the time came to meet at the teahouse. When Shen arrived, they went inside. He insisted on a particular kind of tea and particular snacks to accompany it, but she wanted to try other things too. Outside, rain made a light drumming sound on the lotus leaves in the pond.

"Drinking tea at the open window is so much nicer in the rain," observed Shen.

Ruth flushed with quiet amusement. "We could enjoy ourselves anywhere," she said.

"There has to be something to enjoy ourselves with–a beautiful object, an interesting sensation, a special place."

"You mean like common jasmine we need something to twine ourselves around."

"I suppose so."

"Even something ugly or ordinary?"

"It would not be so for us," he said, his black eyes dancing.

"Even something dangerous?"

"We would overcome the danger."

"You make it sound like an adventure," Ruth said. "Why

can't we just stay at home?"

"After a while we would get bored and dull, then we would not appreciate anything."

"We would savor what we already have."

"How long do you think that would last?"

"I think it would renew itself forever," Ruth stated calmly.

"But tragedy always comes crashing in," he said, hardly knowing the meaning of his words.

They dawdled out past the tourist shops that sold jewelry and love tokens of gold, diamonds and silver and continued back through the streets to his house. Not until they were inside with the door closed did he tell her. They were lying back on the bed, his things all around them, the ceramics, the painting, his other pieces of furniture. He put his arms around her and kissed her. They were already so at home with each other. Then he said, "They want to pull the house down."

"Who does?"

"The city government."

"Can they do that?"

"My brother agrees. My father agrees. I can't understand why they won't fight to get it back. It's the family house."

"If it really was the family house, they would all move in. What can you do?"

"I don't know."

"I like it just like this," she said. "A few beautiful things, and you."

"And you," he added, intently.

"I want to move out of the place where I'm living," she

said. "Can I come here?" She could imagine him saying almost anything, and that anything he said would accord with her desires.

"We belong together," said Shen.

It excited him that she was changeable, energy following lassitude, activity following quiet, whim following deliberation. And for her he embodied a sensation that was there in her all the time, yet also outside her, dissolving the barrier between inner and outer. At some moments she wanted to resist, but she also realized it was impossible to resist a presence so intangible it could take her anywhere.

"Why don't we go out and celebrate?" she said. So they swung their legs off the bed and went straight out.

One day when I returned from business travels in the south, I found that Yun had a new idea. A cousin-in-law in the family had brought home a concubine whom he was crazy about and liked showing off. He insisted that Yun come and meet the young woman.

After seeing her, Yun commented, "Yes, she has beauty but no charm."

The young man was quite put out. He took exception to Yun's criticism. "Do you mean to say that when your husband takes a concubine," he retorted, "she must have both beauty and charm?"

Yun replied, "Certainly. I would settle for nothing less."

From that time on Yun was set on finding me the best possible mistress.

"We are not wealthy and we are so happily married," I protested. "Why do you want to find somebody else?"

At this Yun merely smiled. She wanted there to be no happiness beyond our reach.

Shen and Ruth picked their way down the street, cuddling under one umbrella, unable to keep dry. Love is like the Shanghai rain, a drizzle that forms and unforms in thin air until everything is soaked. Then the rain cleared and in its glistening wake a flame dusk burned across the city, making the buildings loom like dark totems.

A golden dragon stretched above the doorway of the Red Rose Karaoke, blinking its neon eyes. A red rose flashed in its mouth. Ruth and Shen went inside, past the bouncers, down a tunnel into a tangled fantasy of giant roses that ranged in color from candy pink to blood crimson. A few people were drinking cocktails drowsily through straws.

"The place is empty," said Ruth.

"It's early," said Shen. "Ricky says this is the new place. He'll be along later."

A waitress showed them to a table. Ruth slithered along the padded velvet seat and Shen pressed in beside her. The waitress took their orders. Scotch on the rocks, strawberry daiquiri. The light changed their faces, making them look like ghosts. Their eyes were bright, as if staring from an immense distance, their flesh pale as cake icing, exposing the bones beneath.

"You look so funny," said Ruth affectionately.

They nibbled peanuts and watched in amusement as one singer after another took the stage, doing off-key vocals to the jangling music, cheered on by friends.

"You're next," said Shen.

"No," said Ruth, shaking her head decisively, rubbing against him in the banquette, "you!" He kissed her neck and she took the pink parasol from her drink and stuck it behind his ear.

Then Ricky emerged from the darkness with a young Chinese man in tow who was introduced as Black Peony. Ricky's ear stud glinted and his blond hair looked almost luminous.

"Who are you, Cho-cho-san?" asked Black Peony, grinning at the parasol behind Shen's ear. He had bags under his eyes.

"Han is singing tonight," Ricky said. "She's the best singer in Shanghai."

"Just you wait," said Black Peony.

But it was midnight by the time Han took the stage. She had a beautiful face that was made up with thick lipstick and wild eye paint, like the face of a bird of prey. Her body was as tough and lean as an athletic boy's. She was young but could not have told you herself exactly when she was born. She wore fishnet stockings, a black top hat, and a little black leotard that was torn to reveal her breasts. When the lights went down to a single follow spot, the audience leaned farther forward just to be able to see her. When she opened her mouth, a voice came out with a barb to it that could have hooked anything from a baby squid to a shark. She sang to the tinny karaoke backing–that was how she had learned to sing. But what she did with the vocals–syrupy, abrasive, sexy–was all her own performance. Half glamour queen, half street kid, she made well-worn classics and tawdry commercial hits, killed through overexposure, come alive and taunt.

"She's got mixed blood," said Shen, trying to account for the thing that was exotic and indefinable in Han's appeal. The different parts of her body seemed mismatched. Her energy spilled out of control, as if a crazy puppeteer were pulling her strings. She was cheeky, clownish, and mysterious, singing in English, Mandarin, and Shanghainese.

"Where's she from?" Shen wanted to know.

"She's from the streets of Shanghai," declared Black Peony.

"She could be from anywhere," said Ricky.

Shen was fascinated by her mouth as she sang, the way her lips peeled back and her tongue licked at the audience, thick and pink and glistening against the back of her teeth. "What do you think of her?" he asked Ruth.

"She's irresistible!"

Han dropped to her knees to acknowledge the applause, the top of her head all fluffy black duck's feathers. The audience was shouting for more. The manager–a foxy man with a triangular face–announced that the singer would take a five-minute break. Han retreated into the shadows where one of the girls gave her a can of soft drink. Egged on by the crowd, the manager went and grabbed her by the hand and hauled her onto the stage. She threw back her head and laughed with her throat wide open at the audience's love of her. Then she went straight into a Mandarin version of "My Way."

The video screen showed daredevils skiing down Himalayan slopes, shooting Niagaran rapids, hang-gliding off cliff tops above pounding surf. "Dreams too few to mention." Toward the end the crowd was singing along. Han's eyes roved the audience with a predatory smile, noting the newcomers.

People started calling out requests. Shen called out his favorite old Shanghai love song, "Always Smiling." Han noticed the good-looking Chinese man who was new to the place, saw his arm hooked round the fair-haired foreign girl whose eyes were piercing in the light. She walked toward their table and put out her hand. It was Ruth who took Han's hand. Han grinned wildly. She gripped Ruth's hand and would not let go.

"Please sing it with me," Han said, dragging the willing stranger up onstage. She put her arm round Ruth's waist, as if they were sisters.

"What a pair!" said Ricky with excitement.

Shen's request was starting to play. Ruth could keep up with reading the words, but couldn't keep the tune. Her flat, thin voice was no match for Han's. Han belted out the poignant old song, "always smiling . . . in the midst of heartbreak." Ruth stumbled along with a *la-la* that was little more than backing for Han. When they finished, Han gave her a smooching kiss on the lips and the audience roared. Then she stepped out into the spotlight and left Ruth to find her way back to the table by herself.

Shen kidded Ruth as he reached for the hand that Han had held. Ruth's fingers were all sweaty. She fell into her seat, burying her face against his neck with embarrassment. Han was into her finale, the medley of rose songs that led to her signature tune sung in bastard French, in which she mimicked Piaf, placing her top hat over her cleavage as she threw back her shoulders. Ruth adored it. "La Vie en Rose." After Han finished, it was some time before any of the amateurs dared to get up and sing. A stillness followed, a low hubbub of voices that was an expression of respect for the singer.

Then Han appeared again, changed into black jeans and a top. She came over to Ruth and Shen.

"Sorry," she said to Ruth, laughing at her own naughtiness. "Did I embarrass you? You were wonderful. Thank you so much."

"No no no," smiled Ruth, introducing her friends.

"Can I sit down?"

"Please," said Shen.

The waitress brought her a whisky sour. "Cin-cin," she said, clinking glasses all round. Then she glanced in the direction of the manager who was quickly at hand with a cigarillo.

Shen took out his lighter and clicked it until there was a flame, which he held up while Han puffed.

"I'm a naughty girl," said Han as the pungent smoke eddied around the table.

Shen complimented her on her singing, but Han brushed his compliment aside. From his manner she could tell that he was educated and gentle. She asked what his job was. He told her he researched antiques.

"I know nothing about antiques," Han said. "I haven't got that sort of training. I can never tell real from fake. He's your boyfriend, is he?" she asked Ruth.

Ruth smiled. "Maybe."

"Either he is or he isn't. Real or fake?" asked Han.

"We were lovers in another life and we've found each other again in this life," said Shen.

"Do you really believe that?" laughed Han.

"Don't all lovers believe they have met before," asked Ricky, "that it's all in the stars and they have been waiting for each other all their lives?"

"What about love at first sight?" asked Black Peony. "If it's the second time around already, where's the excitement in that?"

"So you already know all there is to know about each other," said Ricky, looking from Shen to Ruth with an edge of interrogation in his voice. "How boring is that. Anyway, lightning never strikes in the same place twice," he concluded.

"I'd be happy for the lightning to strike me just once," cried Han. "Your story's so romantic, but where's the evidence?" she said, looking straight at Ruth and laughing. Her raven eyes caught the flicker of panic across Ruth's face.

Then suddenly Han was impatient. The bar was emptying. "Time to go," she announced. Leaving the others to pay the bill, she ran out into the street.

Shen and Ruth looked at each other, alert to the charge in the air, of desire and play and erotic possibility, and without pausing to justify what they were doing they hurried out after the singer.

Han raced into a side alley where there was a man sleeping on a mat in a doorway. She roused him and told him she needed a car. He shuffled down the lane to his car, unlocked it, and took out a TAXI sign and stuck it on the roof. He revved the car, then turned on the lights and backed up to the club's front door. Ricky had disappeared into the night with Black Peony, leaving Ruth and Shen drunkenly supporting each other in the empty street. Then the taxi door opened, and with a shove from behind Han tumbled them inside.

"Where to, Miss Han?" asked the driver. Then he started ranting about the price of meat.

Han directed him to the edge of Suzhou Creek where there was a little place that stayed open all night for mahjong. The owner said that any friends of Han's were friends of his, but he did not like the look of the foreign woman who might get them all into trouble. He brought their bowls of noodles quickly so as not to give them time to linger. Hands moved, clicking tiles and shifting piles of paper money, raising tea to lips. The gray gambling faces did not move. The driver had a swig of spirits while the others slurped their noodles down and then, as impetuously as she had brought them there, Han ushered them back into the taxi.

This time she sat in the back with Shen and Ruth. Restless, with a belly full of noodles, she was talkative. She liked chili with noodles. Did Ruth like chili? She bet Ruth liked sweet, not hot. That place had the best beef noodles in Shanghai, she said. For seafood she knew another place. Did they want to go there too?

"I can eat like a horse," she said, "and I never get fat except here," she said, lifting up her breasts. "Feel. So much meat already. The more I eat, the more I put on up there while my arms and legs stay like chicken bones. It's because I'm a mongrel. A bit of this, a bit of that. You know all about that, huh?" She turned apologetically to Shen. "Sorry, you want to feel too?"

But when he put his hand out, she slapped it away and laughed some more. Ruth could not stop laughing either.

"Miss Han's grandmother was the most famous White Russian lady in Old Shanghai," the driver suddenly declared. "My grandfather was in love with her."

"My grandma ran a brothel and plied her trade long after the Communists took over and tried to close her down," said Han. "She knew how to do things."

"Is she still alive?" asked Shen.

"There was a rich old trader from Xinjiang who came to Shanghai every year to see her. He was seventy-five when they had my mother. The old boy was pleased to be able to do that. A baby late in life is real good fortune. Then one year he didn't make it back. Grandma made inquiries but she never heard of him again. Then she was sent down to the countryside to be reformed. There was no business in the countryside so the best she could do was to marry off her daughter to a peasant family as a wife for an idiot son. That's my mum. There wasn't much choice. It's my father I'm talking about. Slow, you know.

That's where I get it from," Han tapped her head. "He used to have fits."

Here her story trailed off. "So you have Xinjiang blood?" Shen asked. He looked at her in the variegated light as they drove through the empty streets. She seemed to have the whole history of Shanghai in her veins.

The taxi pulled up outside a hotel and a bellboy in a white uniform stooped to open the door. Han responded to this attention as if it were her right, as if by virtue of who she was she should enjoy the best that the great turbulent city had to offer. She thrust some money at the driver. He thrust it back, refusing payment for old times' sake. But Han insisted, forcing him to relent with a show of bad grace.

She led the way in through the revolving doors, Shen and Ruth flitting after her, the three of them like birds on the wing across the empty foyer. It was three o'clock in the morning. Up to the thirty-first floor and down the corridor to the corner suite where the bell chimed twice before the door opened.

"Han, sweetheart," said Luna Liu, "it could only be you." She was wearing the hotel dressing gown over her silk negligee. "Ah, the lovebirds," she said with satisfied surprise, looking at Ruth and Shen. "I didn't know you knew each other. Well, come on in. Your Taiwanese gentleman has been delayed, darling. Where have you been? I've been dozing for hours. No, I don't want to know."

"Is there champagne, Luna?" asked Han, making herself at home.

"Try the minibar. I'm going back to sleep. I need my

beauty sleep." With that Luna went through to another room of the suite and closed the door.

Han popped the cork on a half-bottle of French champagne and dimmed the lights so they could see the dark sea of Shanghai by night, scattered with luminosity.

Shen pressed his face against the glass. "So much change," he said. "We see it as if we're birds from up here. Maybe when we come to land we'll find even our own nests swept away and we'll have no choice but to keep flying until we fall out of the sky."

"Old things are destroyed," Han said, putting her nose into the fizzing champagne. "Something new comes. Cheers! We're lucky, don't you think, to live in such a time of opportunity?"

Shen was delighted with Han. Ruth was enchanted too. She looked at Shen and caught the dazzle in his eyes. He was not holding her back. No, he was encouraging her to let herself go. She was momentarily perplexed by their behavior. But she didn't stop to question what was happening, or to ask why they were drinking champagne on the thirty-first floor of a luxury hotel in the middle of the night. It was all just part of Han's game.

Han jumped about the room, unable to sit still even though she was yawning from tiredness. If she stopped moving, she would fall asleep, and she didn't want to do that yet. So animated and restless. She held Ruth's hand and danced round the room with her until Shen caught them both and tumbled them down beside him.

"It's hard to get rid of a ghost," Han said. "This hotel is

built on the site of an old graveyard. Only foreigners would be stupid enough to buy that land. There was a honeymoon couple from Hong Kong who stayed up here once. They woke in the middle of the night and saw a man and a woman pressing against the window from outside, all those floors up, clawing at the glass to get in. The honeymoon couple froze. They tried to scream but no noise came out of their mouths. They went straight downstairs and checked out, demanding their money back. The desk clerk said it happens all the time. The old ghosts have nowhere else to go."

Shen and Ruth were laughing, their hands covering their mouths.

"Now excuse me," said Han, going into the bathroom and closing the door behind her. "Ruth," she called, "could you bring me some more champagne?"

Han turned on the gold taps and emptied bath salts into the white marble tub. There was a paneled mirror from the floor to the ceiling. She lowered herself into the warm fragrance, entranced by her own reflection. Ruth came in and set down the champagne glass on the edge of the tub. "Ruth," Han asked, "could you help me wash my neck? It aches from all that singing. Working the mike. Please rub hard."

"I don't know how to," Ruth said, kneeling down beside the bath. There was a puddle of water. "Oh, it's all wet."

"Why don't you get in the bath too?" suggested Han.

So Ruth, without thinking about it, took off her clothes and climbed in behind Han in the bath, and scrubbed her back so vigorously that sudsy water flowed all over the floor.

"What are you doing in there?" called Shen, but they both simply ignored him.

"Your turn," said Han, standing at last and turning Ruth around in the tub. Han could not help laughing at the difference in their figures. Ruth was tall and slender with tiny breasts and a narrow waist. Han was stocky, flat, and straight, except for her breasts, which she held in her hands for Ruth to see. She giggled at how silly she was being. As they tried to sit down, they made a great wave of soapy water that broke over the side of the tub.

Han reached for the shampoo and started washing her hair. "It's a pity to miss an opportunity like this," said Han, opening her eyes to look at Ruth's reflection in the mirror. "Ouch, I've got soap in my eyes."

"You're whiter than me," said Ruth.

"My hair's blacker," said Han. "You should see the color of the water after I wash my hair in it."

"It's filthy," said Ruth getting out. "I'm not going to sit in it anymore."

Han pinched Ruth's thigh, making her lose her balance as she stepped onto the slippery floor.

"Hey," said Ruth. "Watch it." She rubbed herself dry and, wrapped in the towel, opened the door and crept over to Shen, who had fallen asleep on the sofa.

"Who is it?" he murmured, not opening his eyes, touching warm moist skin. "What was going on in there?"

"Han's in the tub."

"You mean it's my turn?"

"Do you want to help her wash?" Ruth asked.

"She can wash herself," Shen said. He dragged Ruth into the bedroom where there was a king-size bed, turned down, with chocolates on the pillow. He put one chocolate in Ruth's mouth and one in his own and began kissing her while she was eating it, so the sensations of kissing and melting chocolate combined as they rolled in under the sheets, Ruth wriggling out of her damp towel to let Shen wrap round her instead. "She won't know where we've gone," murmured Shen.

Ruth giggled. "I bet she finds us pretty quickly."

But Han was out of the bath and was sitting alone in the chair by the window. She felt the soft bleached towel against her skin as she rubbed her hair. She could hear the noises of lovemaking from next door and puffed a cigarillo to empty her mind of everything–all desire, all ambition, all crazy ideas–until she could forget who she was. Fingers ran idly over clean springy skin. She could have been anyone. She could have been anything. And once she knew that Shen and Ruth had finished with sex and were sleeping at last, she tiptoed into the room and found a place for herself at the edge of their large bed. Ruth stirred a little in her sleep. Han sniffed the smell of them. There was a smell of chocolate in the room. Then she drifted off to sleep herself.

They woke with a start when the light was turned on and a man in a suit was standing in the doorway. The porter who had let the man in had turned on all the lights from the main switch. "Excuse me," the porter said, a shiny-faced Shanghainese, peering at the three young people in the bed. They were like the three bears in the children's story. They were rubbing their eyes as the man in the suit glowered at them. He was the real hotel guest, a businessman from Taipei whose flight via Hong Kong had been diverted to another airport. It was his suite.

But before the man could speak, Luna Liu came to the rescue, turning him around, leading him out of the bedroom, and sitting him on the sofa in the other room.

"Mr. Yuan," she said, attempting to soothe her client, "we've been expecting you all night."

Meanwhile she hustled the three sleepy people out of bed and told Shen and Ruth to get their things and go. Ruth found her clothes, wet on the bathroom floor. Shen was angry at being treated so rudely. Han went into the other bedroom to make herself presentable. Luna complimented Mr. Yuan on his new silk and viscose suit. She was good at smoothing ruffled feathers. She made tea for the man and explained that they had been dancing to kill time. They had collapsed from sheer fatigue, for forty winks, nothing more. It was all very inconvenient. When the man settled down, Luna discreetly withdrew and beckoned Han.

Half asleep, half drunk, she came over to the sofa in her slinkiest way. Mr. Yuan was ready for her. Han was special. When she gave him the look that no man could resist, how gratified he felt! He showed his teeth, gold between the stained yellow, and put his hand between her legs.

Shen and Ruth walked home through the empty streets. Shen

told Ruth the history of places they passed, places that belonged to another time and were revealed secretly in the small hours of the night. The yellow walls of a temple that dated from the last years of the Ming dynasty, its black doors like ebony in the moonlight. It had been the center of a soul-stealing scare last century, Shen said. If someone got hold of so much as a hair from your head, they could steal your soul. The district was full of barbershops in the old days and the soul stealers did a good trade there. Shen pointed to the candy-striped poles and the windows plastered with photos of fashionable hairstyles. There were still hairdressers in the area. They stopped at the corner where Shanghai's top beauty salon had stood in the 1930s, where the famous Soong sisters used to go for their permanent waves. Across the road was the park where people still paraded their hairdos, until this year, when it was closed for redevelopment. They looked into the excavation pit that was stepped down like a tomb, where an underground station was being built for the projected new subway line.

Shen had such love for his city. Walking and talking, his hand twined with Ruth's, he seemed to float in a babbling dream as they passed through the quiet dense heart of Shanghai, its streets layered with promises and echoes. Posters for glittering fashions, sleek technology, stern government pronouncements—all jostling for attention and canceling each other out.

Off Nanjing Road they passed the old municipal library, which had been the racing club, with the names of the founding members carved in stone. They skirted the new Grand Theatre, which looked like a crystal coffin. They passed the old entertainment building where Chairman Mao's wife had danced, then approached the quarter where Shen lived, cutting through the grounds of the Conservatorium, which had been the Jewish Club where great families sat down to tea. There, after the revolution, two students returned from Moscow and, under Tchaikovsky's spell, composed the *Butterfly Lovers Concerto.* Shen started to hum the tune, Ruth joined in and they swung their arms down the avenue of plane trees in the first glimmer of a new day.

When they reached his attic, he found the book open beside the wine cups on the table.

"We've been too busy to read any further," he said, picking up Chapter Three and running his finger along the opening sentence.

I was by nature frank and straightforward, for which I eventually suffered.

He set his alarm clock to wake him a few hours later and settled on the bed with the book and Ruth beside him. Shen gave an almighty yawn, which Ruth quickly copied. "You're not going to read now, are you? My eyes are falling out of my head," she said.

Why is it that there are sorrows and hardships in this life? Usually it is one's own fault.

Shen's speech was slurred. The old words carried him off. His eyelids drooped. He was unable to keep his eyes open and was asleep in an instant. Ruth took the book out of his hands, closed it and laid it down. She curled up against him, as if drawing the events of the night around them both like a blanket.

Then she finished the sentence for him, without his hearing.

Usually it is one's own fault, but this was not the case with me.

✵ ✵ This time Stanley came out of his office to confront Shen in front of everyone else. Ricky, feeling seedy, bowed his head. He could imagine how Shen was feeling.

"Is this your idea of a joke, sonny? You say that all the Deputy Mayor's paintings are fake. In a one-page document with no backup. Well, they all heard me roar when I found it yesterday and you had run away like a rat up a drainpipe. I don't know what's eating you, Sean. I don't know what's behind this, but it isn't funny."

Shen blinked at poor Stanley, slumped like a deflated balloon. Ricky stepped in and tried to make light of it. "Oh, this is nothing to how it was yesterday, right, Stanley?" He gave Shen a leery look, prompting him to say something conciliatory.

"Well, it's obvious–" Shen began.

"You're trying to undermine our business, Sean, that's what's obvious. Linda says you're taking a commission from one of our rivals."

"Please, Stanley. Don't listen to Linda."

"Look, it's simple. We need that business. We need the Deputy Mayor's support. We can't get anywhere in this town without it. Zhang Jun is testing us. It's just not right to say those pictures are a bunch of worthless fakes when you could just as easily put five- or six-figure estimates on them. Nobody's perfect, Sean. Nobody's *ever* one hundred percent correct. Nothing's ever one hundred percent fake. There's always a margin for savvy."

"You're the boss, Stanley. I'm only hired to give my opinion. The buck stops with you."

Stanley swelled a little at that. "Now that you've had your little joke, allow me to have mine. You're going to sit down right here and you're not leaving until you've written another assessment on the assumption that these pictures are authentic. Priceless masterpieces. Zhang's coming in with Linda and her niece later on and this time we are all going to have lunch together to celebrate our cooperation. Including you, Sean. Now get to work."

But Shen would not give in so easily. "If you're right, sir, that Zhang Jun is testing us, then what he's testing is our integrity. If we're going to survive in this town, that's the one commodity we cannot do without. People have got to trust us. Rely on us. People who might be tempted to part with their treasures. Art lovers who are willing to pay for quality. Without a decent reputation we won't last more than one season here."

"Are you refusing to do what I say?"

"Yes, sir."

"You won't have a job. I'm warning you."

"Is that right, sir?"

Ricky stepped between them and pushed each to arm's length of the other before fists flew. "Hey hey hey you two, calm down. It's only a difference of opinion. All true connoisseurs differ–"

"Don't you get into this," growled Stanley.

"He's asking me to fake it, Ricky." Shen was shaking with rage. "That's a betrayal of everything I believe in. He's asking me to betray my own ability to discern quality. The difference between real and fake. It may seem like a small thing, but it's the biggest thing in the world. It's what art is all about. And life too."

Stanley was in a corner. Shen's stubbornness set a bad example to his other staff. And there was Linda to face.

"I don't want to make things any harder for you, Stanley. Honest," said Shen. "But this is one thing I can't do. So I'll make it easy for you." A lightness rose through his body to the top of his head and it almost lifted him off the ground as he said the words, "I quit."

"If that's what you want. You're not indispensable. Ricky will do it. Do what you can, Ricky," said Stanley, brusquely handing over Shen's original assessment.

"Ricky?" asked Shen pathetically, wishing that his friend had the courage to refuse.

But Ricky looked helplessly at Shen and his throat went dry. He knew he did not have Shen's fortitude. "I'm sorry," he stammered, walking away with the file.

Stanley headed for his office. Shen stood there alone for a moment, adrift. It was over. He was out of a job. Then he went to his desk and tumbled his personal effects into an empty cardboard box.

✵ ✵ Ruth went looking for Han at the Red Rose, but it was closed in daytime. The janitor was snoozing in a chair by the doorway. When Ruth asked if he had seen Han, he shouted in a voice that carried into the neighboring alleyway and an ungainly little girl appeared. The girl took her a complicated way in and out of lanes, over duck-boards, around a muddy vacant lot to a ramshackle villa where a dozen families had hollowed out spaces for themselves like cave dwellers. What had once been the grand formal garden was a patch of weedy concrete. The entrance was crowded with locked crates and stacked bicycles. In a room at the back crammed with bed, table, television, chests, cupboards, refrigerator, and a fancy little sofa they found Han. Han's cousin lived there with her husband, the girl, and her mother-in-law. During the day Han sat with the cousin's mother-in-law, who was bedridden and dying. Han smiled with amazement when Ruth put her head round the door. The old woman was moaning on the bed. Beside her on the floor was a chamber pot full of dark urine that made the room smell. Han sat Ruth on the sofa and squeezed herself in beside her. Then she told the girl to empty the pot. Han looked at Ruth as if she were a pet—a fluffy poodle or a silky terrier. She did not know how else to respond. The strange foreign woman seemed totally out of place.

Ruth told Han she had been worried about leaving her behind in the hotel room with Luna Liu and the Taiwanese businessman. Han merely laughed. "That's ridiculous," she said. "It's nothing." If she got herself into trouble, it was only because she wanted to.

"Is this where you live?" asked Ruth.

"Sometimes," said Han. "The kid's very naughty, and the old lady groans all night."

The old woman lay against the wall under a gray blanket. Her wrinkled brown face, poking through the folds, was like a fallen leaf.

"I get home late and they leave early. It's fine. They're looking after me. One day I'll get a place of my own."

Ruth told Han about Shen's room on the top floor, done up like a scholar's studio, where they spent their time like two lovebirds.

"That sounds nice," said Han wistfully. "Will you show me?"

Han found an album on the shelf that had a photo of her mother in it, a black-and-white studio photograph with scalloped edges. The woman had a handsome face. "She's still out there in the village," Han said. "She's a widow now. She's got no one else there. I want to bring her back to Shanghai, but first I need a place for us to live. I send her money every month. That's why I never have enough. With a bit of money she can hold her head high in the village." Han spoke matter-of-factly. "A little bit goes a long way there."

"Your life is so complicated," Ruth said. She wondered if her own mother were still alive whether she would have stayed at home to nurse her, whether she would never have come to Shanghai and fallen in love so suddenly.

"How did your mother die?" asked Han.

"Cancer," said Ruth. "Breast cancer."

Han nodded. "You better be careful yourself," she said. "You're not strong."

"You're strong," said Ruth. "I know that."

"My ma said I should go and never come back," said Han. "She said my whole life was a matter of pure chance. People struggled and suffered and made mistakes and survived and I am the result. Free of it all. Free to go and never come back. Be beautiful. Get rich and glorious. That's what I'm about. That's why I don't forget my old ma. She's the only string that's still tied to me. I'm going to make her comfortable in her old age. I'm walking down the road and I don't know where it's going except that I know where my footsteps have come from. It's this life and this life only."

Han giggled. Ruth looked at her and felt a rush of admiration.

Han gave Ruth a little kiss on the cheek and said, "Do you want to go out shopping? I love shopping!"

They strode along the pavement arm in arm. People noticed them as an alluring pair. They symbolized international friendship. Just the sort of thing people imagined for the lifestyle promised by the splendid new department stores of Huaihai Road.

Han liked things of stiff dark material with a military look. Broad shoulders and deep pockets. Ruth liked dark colors too, but in garments that were fine and fluid. They tried on evening dresses and sportswear. In one cubicle they tried one thing after another, modeling different looks in the mirror, flinging rejects over the door until the assistants got angry. Han merely laughed. That was the assistants' job, she said. The store only existed for the customers. Who else was going to buy their stupid things? The assistants wanted things not to sell, so they could take them home as shop-soiled goods.

They tried on nightgowns, pyjamas, and robes. Han fancied herself in a powder-pink robe with a white-rabbit fur trim. She hummed when she put it on, as if she was starting a song. Ruth said it looked so perfect she would buy it for her. Han wanted Ruth to have something too and chose an indigo robe with pearl beading for her. Han said she would only accept a gift if Ruth had one too. Han had no money, so Ruth put the two robes on her credit card, hoping that the account would not be able to reach her in China.

"More paintings will have sold by the time it comes, anyway," she boasted to Han recklessly.

Now that they had started shopping, it was easy to continue and impossible to stop. Carrying their matching department store bags, they headed for the cosmetics counter, where they bought moisturizer and lipstick and mascara and powder. Upstairs above a busy intersection they found a cafe called Les Champs Elysées that had turn-of-the-century Parisian decor and piped French music. Tasseled lamps hung low over the gilded tables and unsteady pink chairs. They sat in a corner by the window that was as high as the billboards and flashing neons and ordered cappuccinos and coffee cake. Their purchases sat proudly beside them on an empty chair, the glossy bags toppling against each other. Ruth said she felt dizzy from so much shopping.

It started to rain. Pink, yellow, and blue in their colored plastic rain capes, cyclists zipped through the crossing below them. The two women felt snug looking down at the slanting water from their cozy nook.

"Why don't you come and live with Shen and me?" Ruth suggested suddenly. "That would be fun."

Han just laughed. But Ruth was serious. The attic would be a better place for Han than the room she shared with the sick old woman and the family with their naughty kid. That was what Ruth gave as her reason. She wanted to rescue Han.

"We can wear our new robes," Han replied with a wicked, mocking twinkle. "I'm sure Shen would enjoy that. Maybe I'll try it for a night and see if I like it."

"Then you will come?" asked Ruth.

"You're crazy," replied Han, skimming the froth from the coffee with her spoon. "Why not? If that's what you want."

"I think we can be friends," said Ruth. She could not say why this prospect made her so excited. The idea of Han coming to stay appealed to her. It seemed to make her relationship with Shen more special still. Although she and Shen wanted to be like a married couple, Han's presence would make them different from most married couples, giving something quite particular to their relationship. Ruth knew Shen would be happier than he could say. "Three is better than two in so many ways," said Ruth in a worldly tone. "You and I can do things while Shen's at work."

Han let her newfound friend babble on. Then she reached out and patted the coffee from Ruth's top lip. Ruth left a tip for the girl in a frilly pink apron who served them. Han disapproved and wanted to take it back, but Ruth slapped her hand.

A bunch of boys with retro hair that was parted down the middle so it bounced like the letter *M* followed Ruth and Han along the street. The boys called out, asking where they were going. "Cat and dog," they called. "Rice and potato. East-West crossover." Dawdling, looking in shop windows, the two women tried to shake the boys. They came across a window full of wigs on dummy heads, all kinds of hair, all colors and shapes, on white, faceless heads without bodies. Han opened the door and swept Ruth inside. The boys were too shy to follow. Ruth and Han stayed there trying on lots of cheap wigs from Russia, giggling until they had chosen two to buy.

Ruth took Han home to show Shen, but he was not there. He had gone out looking for her. When he returned home, he found Ruth and Han waiting for him, both done up like party girls. They had put on their makeup and fixed their wigs. Han wore the powder-pink gown with fur trim and a platinum-blond wig that gave her shoulder-length Sixties-style hair, waved up at the ends. Ruth was in the indigo beaded satin, her hair black and bobbed, Thirties style, with thick bangs that reached her eyebrows. They looked like pinups, poster girls, starlets, bar ladies. Shen laughed with delight. A Chinese beauty and a Hollywood siren. It was a dream come true. But which was which?

"Which do you like best?" Ruth asked.

"Why do I have to choose?" He didn't know whether to play it safe. Either way they would be both pleased and displeased. "These are twin beauties and I'm the happiest man alive. Shall I prepare some food for my beautiful sisters?"

Ruth and Han laughed, hugging each other, and called each other sisters from then on.

They sat at the table and ate the delicious snacks that Shen provided for them, their chopsticks fast and nimble. After they had drunk some wine, Ruth told Shen she had invited Han to stay with them for the night. Shen was surprised, pleased, astounded, apprehensive. But he could not refuse Ruth's whim.

"You're so kind to me," said Han. "Thank you so much. You're both so kind to me that I can never forget you."

Ruth had never been so happy in her life. She did not know what to do with all her feelings. Han prodded her, magnetized her, reached into her, as if she had stolen her soul. She saw no reason why it should ever stop.

They wore their wigs when they went out that night. Han wore her blond wig when she came onstage to sing. Ruth sat with Shen in the audience in her black wig and afterward Han joined them. They sat together, causing people to gossip about them, which only made them feel bolder and more confident.

✱ ✱ They quickly ran out of cash. The manager of the Red Rose gave Han money only when she really needed it and he was very stingy. Ruth had spent most of her money on moving to Shanghai. She had no further income aside from any art sales and her credit card was rejected the next time she tried to use it to withdraw cash at the bank. Now Shen was without his monthly pay, and with no change to their mildly extravagant lifestyle, they were broke within a couple of weeks. And Shen still had his debt to Old Weng for the book.

One day Ruth did not have the strength to get out of bed. Shen and Han fussed over her so much that she told them to go out to a movie and leave her alone to rest. It was just the sort of thing that happened to her sometimes, she told them. Don't worry. She would sleep and she would be fine.

But after they left, she got up and dressed. These days of weakness were part of her condition, the illness she had come to Shanghai to escape. It scared her to be reminded of it and she felt vulnerable for the sake of Shen and Han. She did not want anything to go wrong for them. For this reason she decided to see the doctor again, and when she phoned for an appointment, his receptionist told her to come straightaway because there had been a cancellation.

She chose one of the porcelain bowls that she thought Shen might not miss immediately. It was the yellow one. She wrapped it in newspaper and put it in her bag. She told herself fairly and squarely that it was only a loan. Through Shen she had got to know one of the traders in the flea market whom she trusted to give her a reasonable price. She was too weak to think of any other way to procure the money she needed. After haggling over the amount, she left the bowl with the man in return for some cash. She thought of it as pawning rather than selling. It was strictly temporary. She knew she should have asked Shen, but she could not tell him about her illness. Not yet. Then she went to the hospital, able to afford to see Dr. Jiang.

She was home again before Han and Shen came back

from their outing. The doctor's advice was unchanged. Once again she chose to ignore it. She resisted all medication, all medical intervention. But she had been warned. Instead she rearranged the furniture and took out her paper, brushes, and ink for painting. She painted a couple of versions of the orchid's moon-shadow, then destroyed them because she was not satisfied. She started to sketch some imagined scenes from *Six Chapters,* scenes she envisioned but that were not in the book.

Han and Shen found her flushed with energy when they came in.

"What are they?" Shen asked.

"Scenes from *Six Chapters,*" she replied teasingly. "Scenes from the chapters that are missing."

"How do you know what's in the missing chapters? You mean you made them up?" he asked, and Ruth just laughed.

Han decided not to perform at the Red Rose that night. She, who was so vital, called in sick. She did not want to overexpose herself. She preferred to enjoy spending an evening in her new home. Shen was in a talkative mood and cooked dinner. After eating, they continued drinking wine and he entertained the two women with stories from his childhood.

When I was a kid once I was playing with myself in the garden and I got bitten on a boy's most tender part. They said it was a worm, but perhaps it was a scorpion. I got bitten right on the end of my little thing.

Ruth and Han were duly alarmed as he sat back with his legs apart to make clear the place he was talking about.

My balls swelled up like eggs. The countrywoman who

looked after me was worried it would affect me when I grew up. She was frightened she would get into trouble. The country people from those parts believe that duck's saliva is an antidote to insect bites. That's their remedy for making a swelling go down. So she caught one of the ducks from the yard and held it over me right in that particular place. The duck was quacking and squawking so much that it broke free from her grip and tried to bite me. It nearly swallowed me whole! How I screamed and screamed!

Han slapped Shen on the shoulder. "I bet you were such a naughty boy that you deserved the punishment."

"He's a naughty boy still," said Ruth. "I bet that's a story from the book. It happened to Shen Fu, not to him."

"It's all the same," said Shen. "Isn't it?"

They were laughing so much that no one heard Professor Shen's knock. The old man opened the door himself. He came in and cast a stern gaze over the scene before his eyes. His son was drunk and indulging himself with two strange women.

"Father," said Shen, caught off guard.

"Fuling," the old professor said gravely, dispensing with politeness, "I have bad news. Your brother has been detained by the Public Security Bureau. They're holding him for failing to repay his loans to his business partners. It's a set-up job, but what can we do? They're powerful people and he's a small potato. If we can get some money to them straightaway, they promise to let him go."

Shen disentangled himself from Ruth and Han, straightened his shirt and stood up. "Father, everything I have in the world is here in this room. I would do anything to help my brother Fuming, but my means are limited."

Professor Shen said, "There is no choice but to accept the offer of compensation for our share of this building. Without delay. On the assurance of that sum coming in, I can borrow the money to pay off your brother's debts."

Shen's face screwed up at this. He was filled with pity for himself at having a brother whose ineptitude was causing this last remnant of the family's heritage to be sacrificed. He was ashamed that his own waywardness had led his father to favor his younger brother, who had proved to be so foolish.

"Where is Fuming?" Shen asked.

"In Shanghai Number One prison," replied Professor Shen indignantly. "As soon as I have the means to release him, I will visit him there. On behalf of the family I have already just now signed the document transferring our ownership in this property to the municipal government. It's done. I came to tell you that you will have to move out. You can store your possessions with me. Our apartment is not large," his father went on, "but there's room for you and your things. Your mother begs you not to make trouble. Poor woman. With her eyesight the way it is, she hardly goes out anymore. Your presence in the apartment would make a world of difference to her state of mind."

It was a fait accompli.

"I don't know why our life is so hard," concluded Professor Shen as he headed for the door. "I don't believe I should blame myself."

Shen was shocked. Ruth and Han threw their arms around him as soon as the old man left. Tears came to their eyes as they listened to the heavy footsteps descending the stairs.

"Where will we go?" they chorused.

"There's nowhere," he said. "I've lost my home."

Then Ruth exclaimed, "We can go anywhere! We can go traveling!" She was jumping up and down, holding Shen by the shoulders and making him jump too. "Han will come with us. Won't you?" The three of them, huddled together, were jumping. "We can go back to that little inn on the canal and live like swallows there."

輪

4.

THE WHEEL OF EXISTENCE

They dismantled the antique bed and left it in the attic with some other furniture, planning to deal with it later. Then they packed up Shen's other things, carrying the most precious ones with them, stuffing the porcelain pieces in Ruth's backpack. Shen noticed that his yellow bowl was missing. His suspicion fell on Han but he didn't say anything. At this stage he did not want any more trouble.

In that whirlwind period Shen neglected his reading of *Six Chapters*. He carried the book with him at all times, but he preferred to wait and read it in a leisurely fashion, taking time to decipher its obscure references and oblique hints. Ruth was impatient. She urgently wanted to know what happened next.

She was uncomfortable about letting the story go in midstream. Han, on the other hand, was quite indifferent to the book and her friends' interest in it. She was even a little resentful. Shen said she was intimidated by knowledge, even as she hungered for it. She replied that the book was nothing but a smelly old thing from a dead world. Why should she care about those people? They had not made a success of their lives, as far as she could see.

Together they made the journey to the island of Mount Putuo to pay homage to Guanyin, the Goddess of Compassion, at her legendary birthplace. In the temple dormitory during that trip Ruth started to embroider the Chinese text of the Heart Sutra on a piece of cloth. When Han lit a bunch of incense sticks to hold up before the altar and ask for blessing, the flame flickered so violently in a gust of wind, in the very moment before it burned out, that Ruth took it as an omen and was overwhelmed with desolation.

To ward off any evil consequences Han and Ruth decided to climb the thousand stone steps to the island's peak, prostrating on their knees to Guanyin every second step. They stopped two-thirds of the way at a teahouse to view the silver sea and watch squirrels scampering among the pines. Shen went up to the top of the stairs by the road and met them there. He teased them about their exhausting and incomplete devotions.

Shen was happy traveling in the company of the two women. Wherever they went, they shared one room if they could. Ruth said it would be too lonely for one of them otherwise. They took delight in each other, in the things of the world around them, and in the free, unformed life they found themselves leading, as if their individual existences were merely separate harmonies in a piece of music that was being improvised along the way. They pushed out of their minds the problems and responsibilities they had left behind. It was very easy to do so, as long as they still had a few pieces to sell.

At last they returned by boat to the little canal town of Tianzhou and took up residence in Mrs. Ma's inn. The beginning of autumn was in the air now and the withered peony plant had been put back out in the yard. A large chrysanthemum with tight white fists of buds stood on the windowsill in its place.

Ruth and Shen slept in the big bed in the larger room, like a married couple. Han went to the smaller adjoining room. Sometimes Ruth would wake in the night and sense that Han was lonely, and she would go in next door and curl up beside Han on the bed, and Han's sleepy fingernail would run down the skin of her back. Sometimes Han would be chilly, with the damp rising from the floor, and she would go and snuggle close to Shen, because she said males give out more heat.

After a few nights the chrysanthemum opened into a magnificent flower, its whorled petals, white fringed with green, unfurling to produce a complex, quivering shape, like a tarantula spider dipped in whipped cream. And so too, like a complex flower, their love bloomed.

Shen gave Ruth a bracelet of the best-quality jade, the oldest thing he owned. It had been dug up in a suburb of Shanghai when the ground was being cleared for a housing development. It was a plain circle of waxy caramel-green jade with some cloudy markings in it, incised with a string pattern. After three thousand years it had more life in it than ever. Han was a little envious, but she never said she wanted it and Ruth held back from letting her try it on. Han loved to turn the bracelet around on Ruth's wrist when they sat together, around and around like a waterwheel.

Shen watched them, finding the sentence in Shen Fu's book.

The jade is chosen for its hardness as a token of fidelity and the bracelet's roundness is a symbol of everlasting faithfulness.

"It's a pledge," said Ruth, looking from Shen to Han quizzically.

Shen looked at them both in equal adoration.

Han said, "Who will break it first?" And Ruth felt a quiver of knowledge deep inside that was almost enough to make her faint.

One afternoon, at the close of a lazy wandering day, they returned to the inn to rest. They had walked up to the tea terraces and picked the youngest tips of the leaves, just for fun, and now their plan was to go out to a restaurant on a riverboat for the evening.

Shen took out the book to read. He had reached the last of the four chapters. Ruth dozed, half-awake. But Han was restless. She went out into the courtyard where her voice mingled with the low fluting wind in the bamboo as she sang wordlessly.

I tried my best to comfort her, but Yun could never quite

recover from the shock of being betrayed and her illness returned. Our debts piled up higher and higher, and people began to make unpleasant remarks. We rented a two-room house on the river and I was fully hoping, then, that we were going to have a quiet life and Yun's health would return. But she often cried out in her sleep, "How could Han be so heartless!" and her illness became worse.

I wanted to send for a doctor, but Yun stopped me, saying: "You know my illness started in consequence of deep grief over my mother's death, then it was aggravated through my passion for Han. The illness is now deep in my system and no doctor will be of any avail. You may as well spare yourself the expense. I know you have loved me and been most considerate of me. I am happy to die with an understanding friend like you and have no regrets. Who are we to enjoy such happiness? We have offended by trying to snatch a happiness that was above our lot. Hence our various earthly troubles.

"I have been dreaming lately," Yun went on, "of my mother who has sent a boat to welcome me home. Whenever I close my eyes, I feel my body so light, so light, like one walking among the clouds. It seems that my spirit has already departed and only my body remains."

"This is the effect of your extreme weakness," I said.

"I hope you will find another one who is both beautiful and good to take my place, and then I shall die content." At this point, she broke down completely and fell to weeping as if her bowels had been cut through.

Then she felt for my hand and was going to say something

more, but she could only mumble the words "Next incarnation!" half audibly again and again. Suddenly she began to fall short of breath, her chin was set, her eyes stared wide open, and however I called her name, she could not utter a single word. Two lines of tears rolled down her cheeks. After a while her breath became weaker, her tears gradually dried up, and her spirit departed from this life forever. This was the thirtieth day of the third moon, 1803. A solitary lamp was shining then in the room, and a sense of utter forlornness overcame me. In my heart opened a wound that shall be healed nevermore!

How could I ever express the debt I owed her? I should like to urge upon all the couples in the world neither to hate nor to be too passionately attached to each other. As the proverb says, "A loving couple will not reach old age together."

I'm a case in point.

Inside, propped on the bed, Shen translated aloud. The affecting death scene woke Ruth from her dozing. "Nevermore," she repeated. "She departed this life forever." She had gone pale listening. "And now I'm here. Only why did she have to die in the first place?"

Han ceased her wordless singing and came in now. She looked at them as if she knew exactly the words Shen had been reading out loud. She was jittery and could not stop moving.

Her eyes were like an autumn lake that cools the beholder with its splendor.

"You're not going to run away, are you?" asked Ruth, scared by Han's restless vitality.

"What will you give me to stay?" Han grinned.

Ruth held up her wrist. The jade bracelet.

Han threw back her head and laughed in derision. "You'd give me your most precious possession. I couldn't take that!"

❋ ❋ House lights were reflected in the canal and the voices of people out walking carried far in the stillness. The flicker and crackle of television, the murmur of family talk, the clang of dishes and pans, all merged and softened in the evening air as the odors of the fields and ponds settled at day's end.

The trio followed the canal path to the outskirts of town where stalls and little restaurants served truck drivers and other itinerants. Locals went there looking for fun. Where the canal widened a floating restaurant rocked tipsily at its mooring, the candy-colored lights popping off and on. Inside there was music and dancing. The patrons sat around the upper deck nibbling melon seeds and slugging beer or spirits. Young men stretched their arms along the rail and puffed out their chests. Couples bent their heads together. A spotlight flashed crudely on the dancers. Han could not sit still once she heard a familiar tune. She danced with Ruth, bobbing around the room, while Shen sat and smoked. They were like agitated birds, he thought, of different plumage, Han the more active one, initiating movement, powered by pressure; Ruth passive, following Han, spending energy she could not renew.

The woman who ran the place was a nuggety forty-something. She came and stood by Shen, admiring the girls he had brought with him. "Bean curd and chili," she said, impressed. "Are they both your friends?"

Some men came up from the lower deck, where they had been eating a banquet of tea-smoked salt duck. They settled at a table and continued their raucous drinking game. They all wore leather jackets, four out-of-town businessmen celebrating a deal. They had a couple of local girls to keep them company. One of the men was Sun Da.

"Hey, what are you doing here?" he exclaimed when he saw Shen. Then he spotted Ruth. He stroked his beard wondering if he was seeing things. Then his focus settled on Han who looked wildly beautiful, gripped by the beat of the music in the stark flash of the spotlight, clasping Ruth close as they danced. "Hey," Sun Da yelled, "you guys, don't stay over there. Come and join us."

"What are you doing here?" Shen asked Sun Da as he pulled a stool over to their table.

"Tying up a little business," Sun Da replied.

"But you're an artist."

"I'm an entrepreneurial artist," he boasted, "and our syndicate has struck gold on the Shanghai real estate market."

Shen crinkled his eyes. "I thought the bubble had burst."

"No way," said Sun Da. "You just have to be smart."

The game they were playing involved taking turns to make up a line of doggerel poetry. The first to complete the couplet was the winner and had the right to propose the next line. Losers were forced to drain their cups of wine.

"Flower boat women stir the dreaming sleeper," roared Sun Da, his eyes flaring at the two dancers.

The others struggled to think of a rhyme. Shen raced in

with, *"But when you wake, you're only dreaming deeper."* They clapped him as the winner and Sun Da refilled the empty glasses.

Then it was Shen's turn. *"The old guitar lies mute that no one plays,"* he recited.

The others stammered half a phrase, then faded without completing the line. Ruth heard Shen's opening, broke free from Han and came over to give her answer. *"The silent strings sing of happier days,"* she said proudly, gaining a cheer of approval.

Now it was Ruth's turn. But she was too slow to think of something.

"It doesn't matter," said Shen. He wanted to dance with Ruth anyway. Sun Da approached Han with an offer to dance, his arms spread out like a bear's paws, but she went outside and leaned against the rail, leaving Sun Da to stagger back to his friends feeling rebuffed.

There was a brackish smell around the floating restaurant. Frogs were croaking among the weeds. In the distance a truck thundered by. Han's head pounded, nodding with the beat of the music. Turning and looking back through the open window of the cabin, she could see Ruth and Shen dancing. Ruth's head was resting against Shen's shoulder, Shen's glistening eyes were staring out. He noticed Han and gave her a blissful smile, a smile that Ruth didn't see. Then the song ended and Shen and Ruth came out together to join her on the deck. Ruth reached for Han and the three of them stood holding hands, gazing at the stars reflected in the water, the boat not quite steady beneath their feet.

"Can you see the shape of a heart in that floating weed?" asked Han, pointing at the flotillas of duckweed, shiny in the moonlight, separating and joining, like clouds across the sky. But a tune she loved was just beginning. In a bolt of energy she rushed back inside, wrenching Shen after her.

They danced. She held Shen by the waist, leaning out from him, like a wind surfer clinging to the sail. She fixed her gaze on him, her mouth open wide. She held his shoulders, making their hips sway in one movement, letting the passion between them race like flame along an oil-soaked rope.

Ruth watched from outside, not with jealousy but rather with the fear that Shen and Han would not desire each other enough to be happy. She needed their happiness as a condition of her own. She felt voyeuristic, vicarious, her own pleasure fulfilled in encompassing the pleasure of others.

Ruth watched as Han's long fingers clawed Shen's neck and Shen's hands kneaded Han's spine. Sun Da strode up and tried to break in. He tapped Shen on the shoulder and wedged his swaggering bulk and bristling beard in between Han and Shen, using his weight to shove Shen out of the way, until Shen lost his balance and toppled to the floor. Dreamy drunk, Han closed her eyes and let her body float into Sun Da's arms, like a fish drifting into a net, until she felt him push hard against her. Shen rose from the floor and grabbed Sun Da around the neck, yanking him away with enough strength to dislocate his bones. Shen was growling through his teeth. Han wrapped her arms round her chest in self-protection as Shen and Sun Da swung wildly at each other until they fell grappling to the floor.

The owner came bellowing with a large bamboo steamer fresh from the stove, full of dumplings, and belted the two men indiscriminately as they rolled on the ground.

"Han! Han!" Ruth called. Han skipped outside after her and the two women hurried down the steps to the lower deck where there was a plank to the shore. The plank bounced as Han crossed and flew up and hit Ruth, who fell against the side of the boat, hurting her upper arm. She picked herself up and stumbled after Han down a path to a place where the willow trees grew in a circle, the weeping fronds making a curtain in the breeze.

Nearby was the canal, rippling, catching stray light. They stopped just short of the stone embankment, taking hold of each other, on the brink of falling into the water. Han began turning in the circle of trees, the willows lightly whipping her. She reached out a hand for Ruth to join her. Ruth's arm was smarting. She gave Han the good arm, and they turned until their bodies arched so far back that they could see the sky, upside down. They got dizzy and fell forward and held each other. Han felt the warmth of Ruth against her. She felt Ruth's lips on the skin of her neck. With all her tough power, she pushed Ruth away. Ruth's eyes were burning. She rubbed her upper right arm pityingly. There was a catch in her throat when she spoke. Her voice was heavy. "I am happy when you're near me," Ruth said. "I can't explain it. I don't want you to leave me. Never."

Han moved close to her and touched her on the forehead. A blue spark of electricity jumped across. Ruth shied away, her arms folded round her chest. "See how the energy passes from me to you," Han said.

"It's my life," said Ruth.

Han laughed in her face. "Your life and mine are two different things," she said crossly. She fumbled for a cigarillo and hunched her shoulders against the breeze as she lit it. She breathed smoke in Ruth's face and laughed again. "You're too serious," she said. "This is just good times."

Han was close enough for Ruth to run a tentative hand over her face. "What is this feeling between us?"

"What about you and Shen?"

"Oh, Shen! He's my boyfriend. But you give him the greatest joy."

"Men can't help themselves," said Han. "You're not jealous, are you?"

"It's you," said Ruth, groping for the words. "You set off a reaction. The energy you release binds us together. I can't explain it except that it doesn't come from this world. It comes from a passion that we have already experienced somewhere else."

"So you really buy all that?"

"Just stay with me. With *us*."

Han's eyes could be huge when she wanted them to be, giving a kind of terror to her expression. "I'm my own person. *I* decide. You're nothing to me," Han said.

"You can't explain it either," said Ruth.

Han stepped near and closed Ruth's eyes with her palm. The tie between them came from beyond the limits of both their powers of comprehension. She kissed Ruth's forehead and Ruth put her arms around Han and clung to her. Then, as they sank onto the stone step at the water's edge, they could hear the commotion at the restaurant growing louder.

Han tossed her cigarillo into the water, where it fizzed into darkness. She had Shen's cell phone in her pocket. She called a Shanghai number, but the phone was out of range. "Useless thing," she said. "May as well throw it away." She laughed and simply tossed it into the water. The phone sank with a little plop, no louder than a frog's *knee-deep*. "It was dead, anyway. This place gives me the creeps," said Han. "Are you all right? You took quite a fall back there." She rubbed Ruth's arm.

In that last moment of stillness they must have known they were each struggling with the same thing: you either become trapped in the confusion of life or you cut through it to get on.

Then they heard Shen calling them. There was the sound of his heavy footfall as he ran down the path toward them. He was stumbling through the darkness, trusting his feet to find the way. His shirt was hanging out, torn and bloody. Blood ran from his nose into his mouth and made a dark line down his chin.

Han stood up and called his name. "Shen! Shen!"

At last he burst through the curtain of willows and found them. "Sun Da's going to kill me," he cried.

The women's faces were pale and bright. Shen was gasping for breath. He was hysterical, careless of any pain.

Ruth held him while Han examined his wounds. "All

because of me!" she said, proud that Shen was a fighter. She kept stroking him, comforting him. She said they must hurry back to the inn and find a doctor.

"Are your teeth all right?" asked Han. "The blood will wash off."

Shen ran his tongue around his mouth. "No problem," he said.

They could hear scuffling and swearing as Sun Da and his friends came after them. "So you didn't finish them off, you idiot," said Han, slapping Shen lightly. "Let's get out of here."

They followed the canal until there was silence. "You can trust those girls," said Han. "Those two local girls will lead them in the opposite direction. They don't want Ruth and me getting in their way."

❋ ❋ Dogs barked and people stirred as the footsteps clattered through the streets of the sleeping town.

"Who is it?" called Mrs. Ma, dragged from her bed when they reached the inn. She fetched a basin of hot water and towels when she saw Shen's bloody state, chuckling grimly.

Shen fingered his throbbing nose and thick lip as if feeling the glaze on a lumpy piece of botched stoneware. He laughed to himself, once again filled with that strange feeling of lightness.

"You should stick to painting and books," chided Mrs. Ma as she mopped his face.

"I feel faint," said Ruth suddenly.

They looked at her, just at the moment she fell, and Han caught her.

"What happened?" she asked when she opened her eyes.

"You fainted," said Han. "You're exhausted. We should all sleep."

They put Shen in the single bed, where he could sleep undisturbed while Han and Ruth took the big bed. When Ruth undressed, Han saw the bruising on her arm, a dark mark that spread from her elbow to her shoulder. Ruth stared at it, too tired to do anything, too tired even to sleep, then she felt herself sinking into sleep in spite of herself.

When she woke, she heard the sound of Shen's coarse breathing, through his swollen nose, from the other room. The space in the bed beside her was empty. She had been dreaming that she was floating in deep, formless space in search of her body. Out of all space and time she knew to return to this place, this bed, but she did not find her own body there. When she saw no body in the bed, she panicked and let out a whimper of fear. Then she remembered that Han should have been beside her. She could hear a gentle splashing of water in the courtyard outside. She crawled forward on all fours and looked out the window, her view obscured by the flailing petals of the large drooping chrysanthemum.

Han was in the tub, ladling water over her naked shoulders. How beautiful she looked. She rubbed her skin, lathering, rinsing, wringing out the water from the towel, her shape silvered by the light of half a moon. Ruth watched in fascination as Han turned in the tub, her spine twisting in a slow spiral, the line of her body sideways to Ruth's gaze. Han sponged her breasts, examining them matter-of-factly. Ruth sensed the solidity and weight of the silhouette she saw in the shadowy light. She was close to Han, so close, as if she could touch the nurturing warmth of her breasts and take life simply from such closeness, such longing attentiveness, an attachment as strong as if they were joined by flesh.

Han proceeded in a determined, unself-conscious way, as if she knew she was observed. It might have been that Han was washing not for herself alone. But Han didn't check to see whether anyone was watching. She was absorbed in her task, and once she had finished to her own satisfaction, she stepped out of the tub and let the water run off like rain from banana leaves, as slowly she patted herself until her skin was moist but not quite dry.

Ruth wished Han would look through the open window and see her. From Han's position the window was a black space marked only by the creamy blob of the chrysanthemum. She could not have seen Ruth peering like an owl. Then Ruth was glad that Han had not seen. Delight spread through her body. In that pleasurable inner warmth she lay down on her side of the bed and pulled the covers over her. It would stay her secret.

Shen woke abruptly in the darkness. He inched his way outside and relieved himself against the wall behind the bamboo. Mrs. Ma's rooster, affronted by the intrusion, began to crow, prematurely setting off the other roosters in the neighborhood. Shen crept back to bed, finding the empty space beside Ruth where he usually lay, and went to sleep until Ruth's outstretched arm accidentally landed on his face and squashed his tender nose.

"Ouch!" he said.

Ruth opened her eyes and looked at him in confusion. That made Shen confused too. Then Ruth's confusion turned to fear. "Where's Han?" she asked.

She knew the answer already. In the small hours of the night Han had been washing for the road.

Shen checked the other room. The bed was empty and all Han's things were gone. Mrs. Ma told them that Han had left at first light to catch the early ferry to Shanghai. She had urgent business there, so she told the innkeeper, waking Mrs. Ma from sleep to boil a kettle of water so she could wash before she left.

"We have to find her," said Ruth.

But as soon as Ruth tried to sit up, her head started to spin, the same as the previous evening. Feeling that she would faint at any moment, she eased herself back into a lying position on the bed. "I can't get up. I'm too weak," she said. She looked at her hands and noticed several dark spots. There were more on her forearms, and there was the bruising on her upper left arm where the plank had struck her. The blood had drained from her face. She was breathing in thin shallow puffs. "It will pass," she said. But she recognized the symptoms. With all her will she must try to stay attached to the body that no longer wanted to be her home.

Shen told Mrs. Ma they would need a doctor for Ruth. Mrs. Ma guessed it was a women's problem and said she would cook something special. Shen said they needed the best doctor in town, and Mrs. Ma said he should ask Old Weng for help.

"I'll be back soon," Shen promised Ruth. "Don't strain yourself while I'm gone. Mrs. Ma will look after you."

Ruth hardly had the strength to tell him not to worry. Mrs. Ma's grandson came running in, excited at the prospect of having the foreign woman to himself. The sight of him cheered her up, but Mrs. Ma scolded him and hauled him away. Ruth closed her eyes, but that made her sad. With her eyes closed she could not help imagining Han there. If Han had still been there, she would not have been ill. She would have got up so they could go out and do something together.

✵ ✵ "Ah, young Shen," said Old Weng, slapping him on the back as he ushered him inside.

Shen politely drank tea. The old man, who usually approached matters in a roundabout way, asked directly if there was trouble. He pointed at Shen's bruised nose and thick lip.

"I need a doctor," said Shen, "but not for me. It's for Ruth."

"What's the matter?" asked Old Weng.

"I don't know what's the matter. She's weak. Maybe we've been doing too much. She can't get up. Her arm is horribly black and bruised."

"Oh dear," said Old Weng.

"It happened so suddenly," explained Shen. "I woke up to find that Han, our friend, the singer, had gone and Ruth was ill."

The old man's beady eyes peered at Shen. "The singing girl ran off and your wife took ill? Just as it happens in the book. Don't you see?"

Preoccupied with finding a doctor, Shen had been too agitated to take notice of the obvious parallel. "It can't be," he said. "In the book Yun dies."

The old man nodded knowingly. "You must get her to a doctor immediately."

"How can someone die just like that?" protested Shen.

"She must think the singing girl has abandoned her."

"That was always going to happen. Why does it matter so much?"

"A person can fall over a precipice," said the old man calmly. "They can let their life go."

"Ruth wouldn't do that," said Shen. "Why would she?"

"Yun did so," replied the old man, "because of the singing girl."

"Is Han so important to her?"

"You must read the book and find out. There are certain attachments between people that must be honored at all cost. That is the law of life."

"You mean that Han has broken that law?"

"While Ruth continues to honor it. You must do the same. But know that your efforts may not outweigh this other thing that has sway over her."

"What do you mean?" Shen asked.

The old man rubbed his face from the cheekbones down

to the chin. He paused, not knowing how to start. The topic was delicate. Perhaps his face had acquired its peanut shape from too many years of rubbing, Shen thought as he waited for a reply.

"Scholars still debate the nature of Yun's obsession with Han. You see, it had such a devastating effect on all three of their lives. Foreign commentators, I have heard, label it in a rather crude way. Our great scholars say that Yun merely yearned to experience the beautiful things in life, beautiful things that lay beyond the reach of a well-behaved woman at that time. She was carried away with what she saw in a beautiful sing-song girl. In the same vein she wished to climb all the famous mountains of China too. There was nothing wrong in that, except that Yun had no opportunity to see the mountains; she had too little time and money. In Han she saw something irresistible, a quality different from anything she had ever known, and in that way she allowed herself to experience feelings beyond ordinary limits, in the same heart that felt such excess of emotion for her dear husband. That's all we can understand from what remains. It will always be a matter of speculation."

Shen sat and stared. Slowly the significance of Old Weng's words came to him. "The missing chapters must shed some light on it," he began.

"No one has read the missing chapters, not that I'm aware of. Not since the day Shen Fu wrote them and the manuscript was lost," said Old Weng.

"You mentioned once that you heard a rumor . . . a dealer in Hangzhou?"

Old Weng sighed deeply. "What makes you think you will be the one to find them after all these years?"

"Don't you see?" said Shen, putting his hand to his heart. "Ruth *is* Yun. I am Shen Fu. There is a meaning in our folly. The missing chapters are waiting for us. They will show us the way out of this situation. Now please, old man, write down the details of that dealer in Hangzhou."

On a flimsy scrap of paper Old Weng wrote the information Shen needed. "Beware of him," he added, "he's a shyster."

Shen's mind was moving fast, following all the implications, like filaments, that connected this present crisis to an incomplete past. If Ruth was helplessly possessed by Han, then he was possessed by his need to find the missing parts of the book.

"There is a knowledgeable lady called Dr. Feng, the best doctor in Tianzhou," said Old Weng, returning to more pressing matters, "but her skill may not be enough."

"If she can make it possible for Ruth to travel, that will be enough. We will go straight back to Shanghai and get her into the best hospital there."

"Have you so much money?" asked the old man with irony.

Shen could only grit his teeth, remembering what he owed Old Weng for the book. He would have to sell his few remaining treasures.

✺ ✺ Mrs. Ma gave Ruth a slab of pig's-blood pudding to eat, steamed and soft, mushroom-purple. That gave her the strength to sit up under the red floral quilt and continue her embroidery. But it was borrowed strength. She was feverish as she drew the needle and thread in and out of the stiff cloth, forming the neat Chinese characters of the Heart Sutra: . . . *and so on to no old age and death, and also no ending of old age and death. . . .*

Old Weng acknowledged Mrs. Ma with a dry laugh, like the rattling of leaves, and bowed his head to the young woman in bed. He had a hand-drawn cart ready outside to carry Ruth to the doctor.

Dr. Feng attended to her patients in a bare room at the back of her dispensary. She was a middle-aged woman in a white coat with jet-black pageboy hair. Youthful vitality radiated from her subtle gaze. She examined Ruth closely, noting her tongue, peering into her eyes, taking the different pulses, left and right. She looked carefully at the bruising and the dark spots on Ruth's skin. The imbalances were extreme, the energy broken and feeble, the beat of life almost at a cease. Dr. Feng was in no doubt of the severity of the case, and from the patient's plangent expression the doctor could tell Ruth knew her own condition.

While they were there, Dr. Feng insisted on sewing up Shen's face. He needed a couple of sutures on his upper lip. It was nothing, but it hurt like hell.

Shen asked if Ruth would be well enough to travel back to Shanghai. His thick lip distorted his speech. Dr. Feng said she would prepare prescriptions to support the patient during the journey and a supplementary set of prescriptions to be taken after she reached her destination.

In the dispensary Dr. Feng took a considerable time scooping and pinching ingredients from a wall full of wooden drawers, mixing the medicines in proportion and parceling up the doses to be brewed on successive days. Dried herbs and fungi, bones, insect bodies, roots, shells, seaweed. She interrupted Shen's profuse thank-yous to emphasize her message to the young woman. "Your life is presently in danger. If you follow the precise measures that I have prescribed, you have every possibility of recovering."

Old Weng sighed. Hearing those words spoken with such conviction by the doctor, he had faith too. Then Dr. Feng presented her account. Ruth looked at Shen. Shen looked at Old Weng. Old Weng took the piece of paper and asked the doctor how long she could give them to pay.

"One month," said Dr. Feng. "With a little interest."

"Okay," said Old Weng. "One month it is."

Shen's last cash would go on paying Mrs. Ma, who had come up with a relative, a purveyor of live eels, who was running a barge to Shanghai that very morning. If they could tolerate the primitive conditions, Mrs. Ma said, they could travel at no cost.

The barge stopped by the muddy rubble steps outside the wall of the inn. Shen lifted Ruth in his arms and passed her to the boatman, who carried her to a chair that stood in pride of place under an awning in front of the cabin, facing the bow. Ruth settled in under the quilt Mrs. Ma gave her. The deck was covered with buckets of squirming eels.

Mrs. Ma's grandson sat on the old woman's shoulders and waved good-bye. Old Weng stood beside them as Shen himself hopped aboard at last. His parting advice to the young man was that the book might be their medicine too. In that original narrative was a trace they must follow. Since it was working its way through their lives, they had no choice. It was deep, the old man said. He could not see it clearly himself. It was certain, however, that they must find their way to the true end of the story. That was the path they must follow.

The barge spat puffs of black smoke into the air and churned up the canal as it pulled in awkward, effortful motion away from the bank. Even so, the prow crested a little. It was like a long, low dragon, fancied Ruth. Riding it, she could feel the motion of a wave, as if a layer of herself were lifting. Shen squatted down beside her chair and rubbed her shoulders. Without looking at him, she reached out her bruised arm and stroked the thick black hair on the top of his head.

Ruth threw crumbs to the air and watched the seagulls fight the ducks and the fish for them as the barge moved on and the crumbs sank slowly out of sight. She realized that she would never know the fate of so many things around her in the world. How hard she had tried to push her own fate away, knowing all along that the energy she regained in Shanghai was conjured from nowhere. By letting her energies run past her capacity to replenish them, she had caused something to snap and she was back now in a state of utter depletion, like an empty shell.

She remembered, when her mother was ill in Sydney, moving between home, art school, and the hospital in accord with a spurious graph of progress. Waves of hope crested against inexorable decline. When she was within the sandstone confines of the art school Ruth concentrated on her painting. Alone in the terrace house in those empty spaces while her mother lay in the hospital, she tried to begin a life on her own, as if she had moved out of home already. She imagined the old household cat was her mother's spy. The hospital staff thought Ruth was great–clear-sighted and composed. She had been her mother's one reason for wanting to live. But the best reason in the world may not be enough.

Ruth felt cheated when her mother died. She did not like the story she had been given, with all its twists and turns, leading each time to further loss. But she decided then to concentrate on what truly mattered, as if that way she would be shielded from destruction.

Perhaps her mistake had been to seek out the doctor in Shanghai. The medical world was the same everywhere. She had wanted a safety net, and needed to know what the terms of her condition were. Dr. Jiang had been honest with her without offering reassurance. He had said that the worst was still some way off. The last time she saw him, when she paid for the visit with the yellow bowl, she said it was lack of money that stopped her taking the medicine he prescribed. That displeased him. He said he could not afford to have a patient who was not in a position to follow his instructions.

I thought about the little things on the boat that day. That's what I remember. I could not concentrate on anything else. Our lives are concentrated in so many small, trivial things, yet we turn away from them, always looking in the other direction, for the larger meaning. How often I cursed those inconsequential things—material objects, necessities of life—without realizing how much energy they possess. The wrong key, the missing scrap of paper, the last match that almost flickers out before it lights the candle. Our pleasures are the same. A life of daily pleasures is so insignificant in other people's eyes that it scarcely reflects the pervasive happiness it brings. Yet those little things make all the difference, those stray threads, imbued with all our passions, that bind us, heart and soul, to the physical world and to one another. My longings were tied to a particular person, a face and a shape, a time and a place, but that red thread of passion also bound us to something larger than ourselves. The needle that drew the thread, moving beneath the membrane of our hearts, red as blood, red as fire, was sewing sex into eternity—which is what all lovers want.

That is what I have come to understand, though I did not grasp it at the time.

Dr. Jiang peered haughtily through his gold glasses. His clinician's coat was snowy white and his skin had a supple sheen. Neatly oiled to his scalp, his hair disguised the onset of baldness. His hands rested on the wide desktop in a pose of relaxation. He sighed before leaning forward to take one of the young woman's hands to inspect the little dark spots, the purple petechiae, that had formed there from internal bleeding. Evidently her platelet count had dropped suddenly and the blood was no longer able to clot normally. He wanted to know what had precipitated such a rapid decline. Was she fatigued? Had there been an injury causing loss of blood, an illness, or heavy menstruation? Had she been stressed or shocked or emotionally overcharged?

Ruth needed rest and observation as well as medical attention, Dr. Jiang said. He proposed admitting her to the hospital there and then. When he mentioned how much it would cost, Shen looked at him blankly. There was an additional charge for securing a bed in a hurry, he said. The hospital was already stretched to the limit. On hearing those figures, all they could do was retreat from the consulting room under a cover of polite words. Shen felt useless and bereft. The process of health and sickness, life and death, was out of control.

"Go and find Han," Ruth begged. "Bring her back to me." She was quite unequivocal. "If she comes to see me, I'll get better. Please. I know." She slid from her wrist the jade bracelet he had given her. "Offer this to Han," Ruth said, "and she will come."

❋ ❋ Crowds were spilling from the pavement, outside the barriers, in the way of the traffic. From the plane trees drifted large brown leaves bigger than hands. Always there was the noise, the sudden movement, the disjointed speed of city life. Mothers trailing dressed-up children, bowlegged men wheeling trolleys, women arguing intently as they walked.

Han must be somewhere in all this, Shen knew, moving ahead through a gap, determined not to stay behind. Along with everyone else. Hiding. Lying low. Not even bothering to cast a backward glance. Confident that the big city would sweep her on to the next opportunity.

The manager of the Red Rose Karaoke Bar was evasive. He said that Han had come by briefly before an appointment at one of the big hotels. That reminded Shen of Luna Liu. He saw Luna in his mind, her face distorted by knots of muscle, with some hold over Han's fortunes. He ran out into the road to stop a taxi and hung anxiously over the backseat, hurrying the driver as the gears ground and the car butted through the creeping traffic.

By the time they reached the hotel, the colored lights of evening were coming on, giving the city an atmosphere of weird excitability.

Shen pushed through the revolving doors, past the suspicious eyes of the bellboys, across the polished lobby floor to the elevator. He jabbed *31* and shuffled impatiently as he soared upward. He felt Ruth's backpack hanging from his shoulders.

There was no answer when he pounded on the suite door. A room attendant was pushing a trolley of linen along the corridor. "They've gone out," she said sourly.

"Who are they?" Shen asked.

"An old woman, rich and fat, and a tough little Shanghai bitch, all over a money bags from Taiwan." The room attendant spoke without apology.

"Thank you," said Shen politely. "Where were they going?"

"To eat."

"Where?"

"Try the most expensive restaurant in the place," she replied, rolling her eyes upward.

Shen went on to the top floor, to the revolving restaurant, which was called the Manhattan Room. In a corner by the panoramic window, at a round table that floated above the dark carpet in its skirt of cold white cloth, was Han. She was sitting between Luna Liu and the same man who had found them in his hotel suite in the middle of the night. Han wore a tight-fitting red velvet jacket. In her hair was an arrangement of red rosebuds and gauze. Her face was painted like porcelain. She was a bride.

Mr. Yuan wore a red bow-tie with his black dinner suit, his face red to match from drinking and sheer pleasure. Luna Liu wore shiny gold. They were toasting the double happiness of the occasion.

Shen rushed forward and stared at Han angrily, waiting for her to explain. She stared back at him, oblivious of the accusation he silently put to her. Her red wedding jacket had a high collar of pearls sewn in two tight rows that seemed to lift her head from her body, depriving her face of blood and expression. Her eyes glowered, her rosebud lips were pursed. The exceptional beauty of her face–the possession of which made her bridegroom melt–had become metal hard.

Luna conveyed utter surprise at Shen's abrupt appearance. He looked like a madman. His heart was pounding so violently that he had to put his hands over his chest to still it.

She did not ask him to sit down.

"Ruth's in the hospital," he burst out. He fixed Han in his sights. "She collapsed after you left. Why did you disappear like that? She's going to die because of it. She wants you to come and see her," he said in a pleading tone. It was such a little wish.

Han lowered her gaze, showing no reaction.

Luna laughed. Catching her laughter, Mr. Yuan laughed too, but in a different key, slightly confused.

"You should congratulate the happy couple on their wedding day," said Luna, the go-between, the beneficiary. Behind the fancy costumes and lavish restaurant, this was one of her schemes.

"Han," said Shen loudly, "if you come and see her, she will live. You don't have to run away like this."

Like a flower's head lifting as it blooms, Han lifted her gaze slowly. There was a pleasant smile on her face. She showed no tenderness, no concern. She was glad to be away from the world of sympathy and compassion. She was never going back there–certainly not spoiling her auspicious wedding day for it.

"It's not my fault," she said, turning to her new husband with an artificial smirk.

Shen gaped at her callousness. He and Ruth had loved Han for her impulsive vitality. And now this hardness and control, this exultant killing of all feeling, as if she had simply, brilliantly, switched to another game.

"Well, are you coming?" he demanded, terrified of what

her response would be.

Han looked away impatiently.

"Don't spoil our party, young man," said Luna. "You don't know this young woman. You're mistaken in her. She's very different from the creature you and that dear girl Ruth may have imagined. Ah, the strange ways of the human heart!"

Shen continued to stare in shocked fascination at Han. Was such a gorgeous image of life all steely calculation and unresponsiveness within? Did Ruth mean nothing to her?

"I don't understand you," he said desperately. "How can you refuse to help like this?" But he was merely talking to himself now. He felt the jade bracelet in his pocket. He could not bear even to show it to them. It was all quite useless. He retreated, knowing he must find another way.

Putting his hand in his pocket he also felt the scrap of paper on which he had written the telephone number of the dealer in Hangzhou who had the missing two chapters of *Six Chapters*. But even Shen's phone was missing now. He found a public phone in the foyer of the hotel and punched in the number. The man answered. He agreed to a meeting that night.

✻ ✻ How tired he was from incessant movement! As he rocked from side to side in the night train to Hangzhou, he felt rattled all over. He fretted about Ruth alone in the hospital waiting for the results of the tests and hoped she was sleeping soundly. He remembered the scars on her body. He had counted them one day. The ankle. The appendix. The little one on the chin. He shifted around restlessly on the hard seat, the nylon curtain flicking him in the face, and sipped cold tea from his flask to keep himself awake. He thought of Han's defiled beauty and hated its destructiveness. He knew that if Ruth died, he would go through the world grieving forever. She must not die as she had died in the book. In those missing chapters the answer to her life must be. It was an unfinished story. They were born again to relive what had happened, he, she, and Han, and to complete it according to a different truth.

At half past eleven that night the train rolled into the Hangzhou East Station. When he was a student, Shen used to visit Hangzhou and recite classical poems out loud. He could still remember Su Dongpo's poem comparing Hangzhou's famous West Lake to a woman: lightly powdered or heavily made up, either would do. Hangzhou was a place where people could create their own romance, their own beauty, their own love story, just by wandering about. But late at night it became a gloomy, inert place that he had not the mental spark to bring to life, a businesslike place of closed-up shops and silent carparks, space-age office buildings and featureless hotels. He wondered if Shen Fu and Yun had been there together, or if Shen Fu had gone there for solace, roaming alone after Yun died. That was not in the book, and besides, that old Hangzhou was now long gone.

He met the dealer, a man called Situ, at midnight downtown in the city's most luxurious bathhouse. Shen left his clothes and other possessions in a locker, draped himself in a towel and, clutching the backpack, went through to the area where men lounged after their bathing and sauna were complete. It was glistening and fragrant with steam, but far from populated so late at night. Shen identified the man easily.

Situ acknowledged him with merely a look. He was a blubbery man with flat little ears and big yellow teeth. One in front was missing. He was busy having a pedicure from a wizened old-timer while a young woman massaged the webbing between the fingers of his left hand. His right hand was free to shake Shen's. In a bored, pampered stupor he indicated the reclining chair beside him that was covered with a fresh towel.

Shen could see at once from the thick gold chain round his neck that Situ made money from his dealings and was a presence to reckon with. Like a truffle pig, Situ had a nose for the real thing.

Likewise, Situ assessed Shen in a glance. The fact that the young man had made the journey without pause so late at night, merely on the strength of a tip from Old Weng in Tianzhou, made this the arrival he had been waiting for. Situ was a trader. He had no contacts with intellectuals and scholars. He liked to get his hands dirty, to reach his fingers in and pull out nuggets. When those two worn stitchings of paper came into his hands, he knew that one day the person would also come along who would want them enormously. He had found that person in Shen.

"So you've come from Shanghai?" he asked gruffly. "What's the hurry?"

"I want to know the end of the story."

Situ snorted. "Is that all? I hope you're not treating me as a lending library. It's sale or nothing. I can't let you see the thing otherwise. Would you like your feet done?" Situ offered. "Be my guest."

The old man was finishing off Situ's toenails. Shen had not even showered. "I'm only here to see you," he said. He did not want to be rude, but he did not want to be stapled to the bed by the pedicurist's scissors while he was negotiating a deal. He did not trust the old pedicurist's vision anyway. Peering through filmy eyes, the man seemed to operate by touch rather than sight as he clipped the nails back to the quick.

Shen guessed that Situ's cupidity for certain objects went beyond the strict confines of commercial gain. There was a crass compulsive pride about having high-ranking things in his possession. But a book was different from porcelain or jade, even if there was only one copy. It was about content rather than form, mind rather than matter. Shen hoped that it did not compel the man in the same way.

"I want to show you something first," said Shen, opening the backpack. He unwrapped one of his pair of wine cups and held it up. It was a gamble designed to prove that he knew what he was doing.

Situ's pudgy fingers and softened skin, sensitive from massage, reached for the little cup and registered the special warmth of the porcelain. It fitted the palm of the hand intimately. The man's gold rings and precious stones, clinking against it, looked vulgar and commonplace in comparison. The glaze was *doucai,* contending colors, a design of vines outlined in blue, overshaded with green and red, abstracted against the creamy ground. It was graceful yet finely artless, with a perfection of form and technique that was not only internal but responded in a degree that could not be calibrated to human use and appreciation. Cupped in the palm, the fingers and thumb like five petals around the sides, the rim to the lip, the thing aroused him as he imagined the spill of warm liquid on the tongue. When he put it down on the side table, releasing the object from contact with his skin, distancing himself while still admiring its glow, Situ was already intoxicated.

"The other one?" he asked. "The pair?"

"The two chapters," Shen replied. "Where are they?"

Situ took the locker key that dangled from a damp loop of elastic around his wrist and gave it to the female attendant, asking her to fetch his briefcase. He knew he must make a return move but was quite unable to match the magnificence of the Chenghua *doucai* stem-cup, the pinnacle of Ming. The woman came with a black plastic briefcase and tucked it under his arm. He opened it and brought out the two stitchings of paper, which he passed to Shen.

When Shen took them in his hands, with a bow of his head, he was shaking as if they were holy sutras. Here they were, printed in hand-carved woodblock lettering, the paper thick, brown, and brittle to the touch.

He read the title of Chapter Five: The Meaning of Trees and Flowers. The language had Shen Fu's carefully artless style.

I have always prided myself on knowing every variety of flower, but in Canton I found that almost half the flowers were unknown to me. I asked for their names and found that many of them were not recorded in the *Dictionary of Flowers*. In the Sea Pearl Temple there was a linden tree whose leaves resembled those of the persimmon. You could scrape off those leaves after immersing them in water for some time and reveal a fretwork of fibers as fine as a cicada's wing. You could then bind them into little volumes for the purpose of copying out Buddhist texts.

He proceeded to examine the paper and the ink, but the limpid simplicity of the sentences brought tears to his eyes and he could no longer see properly.

So, after his beloved Yun died, Shen Fu was still exploring the world with a candid, tender eye for detail, as if noticing things for her sake, as if he might one day be able to describe them for her.

Seeing Shen so moved, Situ tried to hit home his advantage.

"Can I see your other cup?" he asked casually. "While you're doing your reading?"

But Shen resisted. "How did these chapters come to you?" he inquired.

The man was gross. His connoisseurship took the form of an intensity of engagement with the physical world, an attachment to things for their own sake. The transmission of Shen Fu's precious missing chapters through Situ's hands was peculiar and implausible. Yet Shen acknowledged that Shen Fu was absorbed in every fiber of the material world too, the world of flesh and blood. Those same threads of material existence joined the author to Situ, and now to Shen, through the rough, fragile medium of old ink on deteriorating paper. That was how the pages survived to be passed down.

During my stay in the south I saw how unspeakably dirty politics was and how low men could stoop in official life, which made me decide to change my profession from salary man to become my own boss. With my friend Chitang I set up a shop for selling books and paintings inside the gate of my own house, which helped somewhat to pay for the expenses of doctors and medicines for Yun. Chitang used to go from one girl to another, "jumping the trough" as they say in sing-song slang. So our debts mounted up. But he was the best friend I had in my life.

The chapters Situ showed him had the very odor of Shen Fu. Shen held the pages to his nose, as if their musty smell would match the fragrance of the words.

"Shen Fu had a friend called Chitang who added to his troubles by spending all his money," Situ explained. "After Shen Fu died, Chitang wanted to publish his friend's book out of memory of the old days. He hoped to earn a bit of money that way. But he turned out to be hopeless at that too. He threw the book together. The pages must have been unnumbered at that stage. They say he dropped the pages and put them back in the wrong order. Chitang went to the cheapest printer he could find, here in Hangzhou, his home town. The printer was willing to be paid as he went along, chapter by chapter. They had already made one rough-proof copy of each of the last two chapters when the printer went out of business for some reason. I guess Chitang was broke and couldn't pay him. Maybe he just died. But something happened and the wretched printer went to jail for not paying his debts. Chapters Five and Six of a book without even a title, a book that no one knew about, sank to the bottom of a pile of old pamphlets and posters.

"They came to the surface only when our West Lake flooded one year and a few chests of papers floated out on the flood and down the road into the garden of a tea merchant who had a policy of finders keepers and kept whatever came his way even if he didn't know what it was. Much later the tea merchant was denounced as a blood-sucking landlord and his property was confiscated. His papers ended up in our municipal archive. Then the archive was ransacked by Red Guards. The chests of papers were old and stinking for sure, but no one knew what they were to worry about, so they were just left in a storage shed that was eventually demolished to make way for the new telephone exchange. The papers went to the rubbish dump and some of them found their way to me. To cut a long story short."

Situ cleared his throat. He pointed at Chitang's name written in small cursive characters in a top corner of the first page of Chapter Five.

"I've been sitting on them. Now, your second stem-cup?" Situ asked again brusquely.

"There are fake versions of the missing chapters around," said Shen.

"You can't fake someone's style," replied Situ shrewdly. "You know what you're looking for. You'll know if this is it."

Shen stared at the lines of print. "I'd need to read it first."

"Do you have any idea what this is worth?" Situ blustered. "The completion of a literary masterpiece. There will be readers of this text all over the world for generation after generation. These pages will be printed over and over again. They are a money-making machine." Situ waved them in the air to show their vigor. "An American publisher has offered half a million dollars. That's more than one Chenghua wine cup, buddy."

Shen shuddered. He could not imagine how an American publisher would have entered into negotiation with such an uncouth man. The pudgy dealer lay before him sweating in a towel that smelled of bleach and disinfectant, at ease here in the bathhouse, a spider at the center of his vast web.

"Let me have some time to study them," said Shen. "Then we can talk."

"Then you go and make a copy and pass it on. I would need something as insurance."

"You can hold on to the stem-cup while I have time to read them."

"One stem-cup, one chapter. We can't talk about more than that until you've let me see the other."

So Shen relented. Taking the other wine cup out of his bag, treating it with the utmost respect, he handed it to the man. Rather than hold it, Situ placed it alongside the other one and simply looked at them. The pairing more than doubled the presence and the value. Perfection doubled and redoubled. Two things, not quite identical, that had traveled together through time, for five centuries now, through the hands of the imperial personage and the consort who drank with him. By matching, distinguishable one from the other, if only barely so, their perfection was enhanced. They partnered each other still, containing their secrets, as the two observers joined in one gaze. Situ was in awe, filled with covetous lust. But sensing Shen's unstoppable desire for the book, he relaxed. He and this ardent young man were matched too. They had something to trade.

Situ said, "If you can ever prove that the chapters are fake, I will give you back the cups. I promise you. Is that a deal?"

In any case Shen knew he had no choice but to take the opportunity that was offered. Thinking of Ruth, he could not allow himself to reconsider. There was no time.

The two stem-cups stayed resting on the table. Shen remembered the day he found them, wrapped in oily cloth in the back of a drawer in the house of an old lady who used to play with him when he was a child and who simply disappeared one day, a political victim. They were her indirect gift to him.

Situ picked up the second one and was holding it in his palm now, squeezing it against the cushion of his flesh. Shen stuffed the two chapters into his bag with no further ceremony and adjusted the towel around his naked body, keen to be on his way. He did not want to think about what he was doing, his precious Chenghua stem-cups, the finest pieces of their kind ever likely to exist, cast away in this sticky perfumed chamber to the sound of steamy water endlessly gurgling and gushing, the place already past the heyday of its brief glory.

Yet he knew what he was getting in exchange. He was the one destined to find the answer to the puzzle of Shen Fu's book of life and love, left remaining for two centuries to those who came after. In it he would also find the answer to his own life, and Ruth's, the woman he loved.

Situ did not even rise when Shen stood and stretched out his hand. The man was nestling the cups in the hollow formed between his two flabby breasts. Without unbalancing himself, he reached out a soft hand to shake Shen's. He was grinning. He was satisfied. In that moment the two men's lives, their cleverness, their folly, their triumph, wove perfectly together into one twist of thread.

花

5.

THE SINGING GIRL

According to custom, the spirit of the deceased is supposed to return to the house on a certain day after a death has occurred. People arrange the room exactly as the deceased person left it, putting old clothes on the bed and old shoes by the bedside for the returning spirit to take a farewell look. Priests are invited to recite incantations calling to the spirit to visit the deathbed and then sending it away. The custom is to prepare wine and dishes and leave them in the dead one's chamber.

My friends urged me to leave the offerings at home and get away. To this I gave a cold, indifferent reply, for I was hoping to see the spirit of Yun again.

"To encounter the spirit of the deceased on its return

home has an evil influence on living men," they said. "Even if your wife's spirit should return, she is living in a world different from ours. You won't be able to see her."

But I was so madly in love with her that I did not care.

I went in with a lamp in my hand and saw the room exactly as she had left it; only my beloved was not there. Tears welled up in my eyes in spite of myself. I was afraid then that with my wet eyes I should not be able to see her clearly, and I held back my tears and sat on the bed, waiting for her appearance with wide open eyes. Softly I touched her dress and smelt the odor of her body, which still remained, and I was so affected by it that I lost consciousness for a moment or two. Then I thought to myself, How could I let myself doze off since I was waiting for the return of her spirit? I opened my eyes again and looked round and saw the two candlelights burning low on the table, as small as little peas. It gave me goosebumps and I shuddered all over. I rubbed my hands and my forehead and suddenly the glow of the flame illuminated the whole room and enabled me to look around clearly. Secretly and in a quiet tone, I called her name and prayed to her, and I saw the flames of the candles leap higher and higher till they were over a foot long.

People were asleep all around him, wrapped up in padded coats, heads bent forward, as the train rumbled on its dawn way toward Shanghai, and Shen continued reading. Feeling her there yet having no word but the sudden flaring of the candles into tall flames, it was not so different from the longing with which he thought of Ruth in the hospital. With the same desperate anxiety, he imagined her moving beyond his reach. He willed the train to race faster on its tracks through the dim fields and obscure stretches of expanding suburbs. Her life was waning even as he journeyed. He urged the clanking wheels to close the gap between him and her. Like poplar trees on fire, the candles flared in his inner vision, making him shiver with fear, as if in the exhaustion of his own body he were already experiencing Ruth's death.

But no, that was not what the rediscovered pages of the book said.

I bought a grave plot outside the West Gate on Golden Cassia Hill and buried Yun there. The graveyard keeper said to me, "This is a propitious place for burial. The spirit of the earth is strong."

I secretly prayed to her: "Oh Yun! The autumn wind is blowing high and my gown is thin. If you have any influence, please protect me. . . . "

While I stood by her graveside, dressed in my white robe of mourning, I heard a commotion at the bottom of the hill. A young woman was running wildly about in the company of a group of monks who were leading her to the grave. She broke away and ran ahead of them. Her hair was in disarray and her clothes were torn and dirty. Her bare arms were black and blue. When she got closer, I recognized Han. Her face was raw from crying. The sight of me only increased her tears. She ran past me distractedly and threw herself on Yun's grave, sobbing violently. The monks gathered around her and let her weep, before pulling her to her feet and attempting to calm her. She was quite hysterical.

"Yun! Yun!" she cried. "You should not have died. You were too full of love." Then she started beating her breast with clenched fists.

I was startled by the disturbance at the graveside. Yun would probably find it nonsensical to expend so much passion on something that was beyond remedy. But Han could not stop her laments. She was so full of self-accusation and remorse. She had come back too late, and now Yun was dead. If Yun had known of her loyalty, she would never have fallen ill and died. That made it unbearable.

The rich man who married Han had treated her like a slave. Her place in his household was lower than a dog's, so roughly did he use her. She could not tolerate the situation another day. But she knew if she ran off, he would send men after her to beat her and bring her back. Remembering the happy times she had enjoyed with Yun and me, and the great devotion Yun had shown her, she was filled with the bitterest regret.

She asked the members of the household for news of us. When she heard that Yun had died, she was aghast, and when she was told that I was keeping vigil by Yun's graveside, she crept out of the rich man's bed in the middle of the night and made her escape. She found the monks who were responsible for that graveyard and asked them to take her straight to Yun's burial place. The monks told her what they had heard of how

Yun died. A sworn sister had abandoned her when Yun expected the two of them would stay together for the rest of their lives. So Han learnt it was her betrayal that killed Yun.

The monks guessed that she must be the girl in question. As they led her to the grave, she rushed ahead of them in a frenzy. When she saw me, my look of cold scorn showed her in a glance that what she had heard was true. Her sudden absence had caused Yun to die. There could be no other explanation for something so strange.

Smoke rose from the burning offerings by the grave mound on the hillside, disappearing into thin air. So all our spirits, our feelings, our passions, dissolve and disperse. Han screamed when the monks tried to drag her away at nightfall. She refused to leave Yun's side, even as the rain came on and the ground turned to mud. She believed that her love for Yun must be strong enough to bring her back into this world. Otherwise she would join Yun and drift into emptiness. I begged Han to leave Yun's spirit in peace.

Later I applied for a job as secretary to a county administrator in a remote little town and tried to earn enough money to repay my debts. So I continued my life, occasionally finding a moment of pleasure in a moment of forgetfulness.

I heard that Han never returned to the rich man nor to her old life as a singing girl. She roamed into the mountains, begging for her food and shelter in poor villages, sometimes working as a prostitute until she was too skinny and dirty even for that. I heard that at last she found refuge in a Buddhist nunnery. So the wheel of existence turns.

Shen sighed, rubbing his tired eyes. He recognized the scenes outside the window now, familiar streets seen from the railway tracks, tenements, little rooms hung with laundry, sooty balconies massed with potted plants. He had no sympathy for Han. He had enjoyed her, but he had never felt deeply for her, and now he did not want her to survive unscathed. He could not fathom the intensity of Ruth's attachment to her, which seemed to have arisen from nowhere, and what he could not fathom he was inclined to resent. On the other hand, the book was his guide and it held open a slim possibility of hope. He could not give up on Han yet.

After many years an old master visited the temple where Han was living. When he interviewed her, he asked why she continued to live a life of austerity and sacrifice in a condition of such suffering. She explained that her heart had been raw and ferocious, that she had loved both too much yet not enough, that she was intent now on burning her passion away as an incense stick burns to ash. She wanted only devotion to Yun's memory to be left in her, a mirror of Yun's devotion to her.

Bound to atonement, Han longed to purify herself until the thread of her shame could be cut and the spirit world was all that remained, a pure emptiness that matched Yun's innocence in her brief, sweet life.

On the contrary, the master said, Han's devotion to Yun was having the effect of keeping the connection between them alive. Her unending sorrow and endurance for Yun's sake, and for the sake of her grieving husband (so the master said), and for herself, only bound the three people together, tying them helplessly to the passing world of heat and light at the same time. The master said the only way to end the tie was to follow the thread until the passion of attachment reached its final resolution. Then there would be a chance for release from the residue of pain that she had caused.

The master, almost fleshless himself, surprised her with his analysis. The power of passion refined into its purest energy, as he witnessed it in Han, was enough to make him turn his usual ascetic wisdom upside down. Han had earned herself another time around in which she would know how to honor the feelings that arose in our hearts.

In hearing his words, she was released from her vows and returned to a life in the world.

Han had run off, Shen understood, but she came back. The timing would be different this time. The power of the participants to act out their hearts' truths would be different. They would know themselves now and act with courage. Han would realize what she had done in giving herself to Mr. Yuan and repudiate her own turbulent motives. She would return to Ruth, and Ruth would live! Shen was clear about that. Anything else would only perpetuate misfortune. Han had one more chance to release them all, including herself, from the terrible weight they had carried for so long. The way was open, Shen knew, for Han to act, to come to Ruth, to reciprocate her devotion. There was no other choice. The content of the missing chapters authenticated everything.

He remembered one of the pictures Ruth had drawn–of Han with shaven hair weeping over Yun's grave.

He fingered the paper, confirming what he had hoped for, blind to everything except the pattern that the pieces of evidence formed in his mind.

Outside in the steely blue light of a new day the train slowed against the platform. Shen was quick to open the door and jump down. His obligation was to persuade Han to return. Thinking of her cruel face and burning eyes he could almost begin to desire her again, to be excited by her defiance, to admire her splendid self-seeking beauty . . .

. . . powdered like white-washed walls and rouged like fiery pomegranate flowers.

✺ ✺ Shen took a bus from the station in the direction of Han's hotel. He got off at an intersection where he could see the hotel looming like a monument, dark except for a few eyeholes of yellow where sleepless guests had their lights on—sparse, scattered dabs of light that formed a minimalist pattern on the hulk of the building. He remembered Han talking about the distraught ghosts that clung to the outside of those windows during the night, trying to find a way back in. He hoped they were dispersing now as day came near. The lights were on in the suite at the corner of the thirty-first floor, he could see, and the curtains wide open.

He knocked, but she ignored his knocking and only opened up when he called her name. She gave him a sullen stare, drained and savage, as if she had nothing left but her instinct of self-protection. Then she reached for his wrist and pulled him inside. The furniture was strewn at odd angles, doors and drawers flung open, as the pallid light thickened over the river in the distance.

Shen asked where the gentleman was, her husband, Mr. Yuan. Han laughed sourly. She was feeling the effects of drinking and smoking all night. The man had left already for the airport to catch an early flight back to Taiwan. He was not a husband but a *Taiwanese* husband, she said. He had a number one wife back in Taipei. Han was his number two, his Mainland wife whom he could treat like a cheap investment that might pay off one day. He had asked her not to see him off at the airport because he wished to avoid a scene. She waved the spectacular diamond ring through the air as she told her story. It was her trophy. Now that the honeymoon was suspended, Han faced the truth of the situation Luna Liu had talked her into. The man had treated her like an animal on the wedding night, without respect or gratitude, and already he was on his way, another business traveler, before the sun had time to come up. Han was left behind to wash herself down, dress herself up and walk out through the lobby with whatever dignity she could muster. The staff would clean, air, and make up the room, put flowers in the vase and fruit in the bowl ready for the next guest. The little drama might never have happened, except that Han was richer and had a diamond ring to show for it, and the man was bound to come back for more, as the keenest customers always did. But the price would get lower each time until in the eyes of those who watched her leave the hotel in the mornings, she might as well be back on the street with the starving flesh of the common people.

Han pushed a drink into Shen's hand. He would have preferred hot water. In return he poured water over a tea bag in a glass for her. "Sit down," he told her. "Calm yourself. Listen."

Cocking her head to one side, she came over and clinked her tea glass against his whisky to make him drink. She put an arm round his neck. "Relax," she said tenderly. "You look crazy. Take your shoes off. Stretch out on the sofa. What are you doing here anyway? It's five o'clock in the morning." She gave him a little peck on the lips. If she tried to seduce him, he would probably succumb to her invisible fire. As she came closer he could feel it coiling around him. He would have liked nothing more than to yield, abandon himself to his bond with Han, that mutual recognition of carnal attraction, but he resisted.

He put down the whisky without tasting it and took hold of her hands. "No," he said, redirecting her energy, "we can comfort ourselves later. There is something more important I have to tell you. I have been traveling all night. I have been to Hangzhou. I have found the missing chapters."

"That book!" Han screamed. She catapulted herself across the room toward the windows as if she was going to plunge right through the wall of glass.

"Han," he continued, "you will be cursed through endless cycles of existence unless you take notice of what I'm saying. You ran away of necessity but you always planned to come back. You were always loving. You were always loyal. You did not mean to cause anyone's death. When you found out what had happened, you were stricken with remorse. In the old story you showed such devotion that you were granted the power to bring us all back into this world with a second chance. You, Han. Don't turn your back on that now."

Han stood close to the window, her arms folded, her hands gripping her elbows, hiding from what he said. "You're crazy," she shouted. "Leave me alone. I can't do anything about Ruth."

"I want you to come and see her; that's all." He spoke calmly, as if coaxing a frightened, cornered creature. "Your heart was wild then. You destroyed love. Then you recognized your mistake and made amends. Come and see Ruth who loves you. Come, and you'll save her. Then you'll be free. It is the last step."

Han cringed from him. "You'll never let me go," she cried in a rasping voice. "Look out there." She was staring out at her city. "I want my place in it. It's okay for you, Mister Shen. You've got education, you've got background. You've got a bright future as a family man. You have your place. As for that loony foreign girl, she's sick. She's frail. She's a dreamer. Let her have a good time while it lasts, but leave me out of it. That's death. It's disease. She's a beautiful sweet flower. Pick her and she's gone. I'm not giving up my opportunities for her. I don't owe her or you anything. There never was any deal. We had our good times. Now let me go. Up here is my place, not down there on the street. My husband has promised me. A diamond ring every time. That's fine by me. So, good-bye."

She ran her hands over the glass, speaking to the murky rising day, clawing for a place in the material world like one of those stranded restless ghosts.

"Even if your heart's not in it, maybe you can go along

with it, just this once. You're a performer, after all."

"No," she said.

"Are you worried," he asked, "that what I'm saying really is your destiny?"

"What's in it for me?"

"You'll be burnt to a charcoal stick if you fight this. Release yourself."

Then she turned around and faced him. "I don't believe in the book. It has no value to me. I only believe what I can touch and eat."

Shen reached into his pocket and took out the jade bracelet. It was a chance find of the earliest known civilization to exist on the marshland that had become this city, from three thousand years ago, and the quality of its jade was incommensurable with any other. He moved toward her, holding the jade circle in his hands, slowly, step by step, reading her as he did so, and when he was just in front of her, he fell to his knees and bowed his head to the floor.

She tossed her head back and scoffed.

Shen held up the jade bracelet in his hands, offering it to her in an act of obeisance. "I beg you."

Like a monkey grasping at a shiny bauble, she could not stop herself reaching for the warm caramel-green jade, with its incised lines, countless ages old. She had turned it longingly on Ruth's wrist. She had it in her own hand. She had it around her wrist. How it appealed to her, that ancient, valuable talisman of life. It was understood. It was a deal. She would come.

✷ ✷ After Shen left, muttering good-bye as he backed awkwardly from the room, Han crumpled to her knees on the floor in horrified mockery of his kowtow. "I beg you," she moaned to herself, repeating his words over and over until she began to cough, "I beg you." She clutched her belly, retching at the thick carpet of the hotel room until she felt her body empty itself completely, her chest folded against her bent legs. She was nothing more than a bag, crushed and flattened to the ground. So this was emptiness, this was nothingness, this was how it felt when the attachments of the world were severed and there was only aversion. There was nothing but her own torments, unless she could break the cycle in which she had been turning. That was what Shen had come to show her.

It was not his truth, of course, nothing to do with him. He was merely the channel. And the pages of the book were little more than ash in the wind. The truth came from the point where she was joined to the larger world of spirit and law, where the link of compassion was made. In another life she had cut the cord at that point, but some last sinew had stayed, an invisible thread that pulled her back. She pressed the jade bracelet up her arm, making it squeeze her flesh. She splashed cold water on her face. Her eyes were puffy. Her skin was sallow. She felt nauseous. She put on the high-heeled black sling-backs that went with her black jeans and sleeveless black top. She was going not in poor cloth shoes, not in mud, but with a gold chain round her neck, a diamond ring on her finger, and the jade bracelet on her arm.

As she lay in the dim hospital room, Ruth thought only of Han. Alone, with her eyes closed, she felt the soft skin of her belly and the velvety inside of her thighs, imagining it was Han's skin, close to her, sweet and moist. She felt her breasts and they were Han's breasts. The memory reached inside her body like insistent fingers, forcing her to yield, even as she lay silently trying to drive away the thought of Han. Ruth knew she would die of the pain.

She changed position in the bed, exhausting herself by tossing over and over, as if that would make Han disappear. All the time she was longing for Han to be there, to touch her, to hold her, to laugh with her, to be her secret sister once more. She willed her longing dead, she willed Han dead, she willed herself dead as the only means to kill the pain. She thought of Han's black lips and teasing eyes. Pressing her own wet tongue against her teeth she imagined Han's tongue, pointing its tip at her. She cursed the hand that had gripped hers that first night and pulled her up onstage. If only she had refused.

She remembered how Han had shoved her away, under the willow trees in Tianzhou, then clutched her in comfort. She saw Han washing herself in the moonlight. Running her damp fingers down her breastbone, she was washing Han herself. Then she turned over and lay with her mouth smothered against the sheet. She wanted to die. Han had left her, betrayed her, taken her life away. She was nothing, she was worthless, she wished she could stay buried in the hospital gloom forever. Then she groaned and the nurse came running.

"Get this thing off me," Ruth said. The nurse, who did

not know what she meant, began adjusting the bedding. But Ruth meant the animal that clung to her heart, its claws in her flesh, squeezing the very pulse of her existence: the dark-haired, wide-eyed creature of the night that she called Love.

✵ ✵ Ruth's face glimmered palely when Shen walked in the room. If he was there, nothing could matter so much. She was tired and weak. She had tossed and turned all night. She had come to an understanding with the nurse to boil her herbal medicine, although it was against hospital practice, and she sat up in bed sipping it, hiding the mug under the snow-white mound of the sheet.

So much of the happiness in her life had been created in the glow of other people's dreams, she realized. It was not until she met Shen that she found her own happiness. And then she met Han, and the old impossibility returned, the dependency on others whose lives were beyond her reach.

"Did you see her?" Ruth asked.

"I gave her the bracelet."

Shen wondered if he should tell her about finding the last two chapters of the book–the book that promised Yun a second chance to live if only Han could learn faithfulness of heart. Han had wanted the jade bracelet so violently, but there was no guarantee that she would come, and now they had nothing else to offer her.

Dr. Jiang came in with the results of the tests. He was displeased to see Shen there so early.

"Visiting hours are in the afternoon," he said, shaking

Shen's hand with a blank smile, then changing to an expression of worry as he turned to Ruth. "Excuse me," he said, taking Ruth's hand in his. He pulled a needle from his pocket and pricked the cushion of flesh at the base of her palm. A droplet of blood oozed out. Looking at his watch, the doctor dabbed it with a tissue. After three minutes it was still wet. Satisfied with his experiment, Dr. Jiang looked from Ruth to Shen. "You see, the blood's not coagulating. Any serious bleeding and you'd be in trouble. You risk hemorrhaging." He read from his notes. "The blood platelet count is down. Other symptoms of an autoimmune response are manifesting. The ITP is at an advanced stage. The best solution is a splenectomy. Surgical removal of the spleen."

Ruth ran her hands over the bedding in silence.

"Are you sure?" asked Shen, incredulous.

"It's the textbook treatment," said Dr. Jiang, not bothering to explain further. "I don't see that you have much choice. If it works, you'll be a winner." He did not complete his sentence by saying what would happen if it did not work. "We'll need permission from the next of kin before we can operate."

"That would be my father," Ruth said. "He's in New Caledonia."

"And what are your charges?" asked Shen, standing in the doctor's way.

"It's a complex procedure, of course. The first step is to see when I can book her in for surgery. Don't worry. We're well equipped to do it here. You're in the best possible hands."

Dr. Jiang's reassurances as he left the room made Shen more anxious.

"Surgery!" Ruth shook her head. "That's exactly what they said in Sydney. Remove the spleen. It's a useless organ anyway."

"Then you knew?" Shen ventured.

"I came here to get away from it," Ruth said. "And here I am, no further ahead."

"Here *we* are," said Shen.

"Please," said Ruth, "you'll have to call my father and tell him. I'll write down the number."

He came over and kissed her on the lips. She purred. He stroked her forehead until she closed her eyes, soothed by his care. Then she opened them again and sat up straight. "I don't want the operation," she said. "We can't pay for it anyway. There's nothing left for money. Shen, I never told you–the yellow bowl. I pawned it in the flea market. It wasn't Han, it was me who did it."

"Even then you knew?"

"Yes. And now there's only your pair of stem-cups left and you're not selling them."

"The stem-cups have gone," Shen said bleakly, "in exchange for the chapters."

Ruth moaned. "No. They were worth more than that. More than me."

✷ ✷ "Is that Mr. Garrett? I'm sorry, do you speak English? I'm calling from Shanghai, China. I'm a friend of your daughter–Ruth." Shen stood in the hospital corridor shouting into the phone. "My name is Shen."

The voice was unfamiliar down the distant line against remote background crackle. Echoing, the two voices kept colliding.

"Where is Ruth?" the man asked. The sun was shining where he was. His hair was wet and combed down after swimming. He had trouble turning his mind to this intrusion into his morning. A minute before he had been cursing the local politicians for not demanding enough from France when Paris was on the back foot and willing to agree to more, much more, for the sake of harmony in the independence referendum. No one pushed hard enough, Luc always said. His shirt was open and he ran his hand in agitation through the sweaty hair on his chest. His new wife, Laura, was frying up onions and chili, making him hungry already for the midday meal. "What do you say?"

"Quoi?" she called out through the sizzle and smoke.

"Ruth's in the hospital. In Shanghai," Shen shouted into the phone. "She's in critical condition. She needs an operation. She needs your permission."

"Why is she in Shanghai? She should be back in Sydney if she needs to go to hospital. We can come to Sydney. How can we come to Shanghai? Who are you, anyway?"

"Please, it's an emergency. We need your permission. My name is Shen."

As he listened, Luc Garrett felt the ties of blood rope him in. He had always known there was a point at which his daughter would come back to claim him, when the past, his ex-wife, his dead wife, would exact a toll that he could not refuse to pay. The fellow on the phone was saying that she had a blood disease and that the doctor proposed to cut out her spleen in an attempt to save her. Luc had been waiting–and now this was it.

"Tell me exactly where she is," he said.

"So you will come," clinched the voice.

A prankish Pacific wind rattled through the palms and the banana trees and flushed the purple clusters of bougainvillea around the house. Then the wind dropped, dying down into the settled silence of the hour before noon.

"What is your relationship with Ruth?"

"I am her best friend," Shen said.

"Thank you," said Luc. "Do you need my permission in writing?"

"There's a form I can fax you."

"I'll let you know our plans. *À bientôt.*" Then Luc hung up.

He turned to Laura and told her the news. He put his arms round the woman's waist and rested his forehead against hers. He was compelled at last, by signing a form, to be his daughter's father.

Ruth wondered, as she lay in the hospital bed, how absence could make the sense of another person so intense, as if their reality came from the yearning you felt inside yourself. Could the other person be unaware of such feeling? It squeezed her body as if a sculptor were molding wet clay. How could they continue their way through the world not knowing the shape of passion that was pressing around them? How could they not respond?

Soon the anesthetist would be coming. Ruth wondered what love could be other than pain. It hurt to love the absent form of Han, but Shen hurt her too, if she could not have Han. She tried to calm herself, wishing her feelings would go away. Yet there was nothing else. She screwed up her eyes. Again the turmoil of desire seized her body. It would only end when Han gripped her hand. Or when she ceased to exist.

✷ ✷ Shen made the long bus ride to the university campus, where his father lived. In his student days, when he lived with his parents, he used to take the bus into the city to haunt the bookstores and newsstands, to meet people or just look for the thing he needed to direct his next steps, the clue to follow in search of the secret of his life. He had never known what it was, not until he met Ruth and, falling in love with her, fell into his destiny too. He owed her the finding of himself, which was everything.

Professor Shen smiled wryly at his son and brought him through to the sofa where he could sit beside his blind mother.

"I always know you by your smell," she said, feeling his face in a way that was at once tender and precise. "You smell like burning aloes–pungent and musty."

"Don't, Ma," he said, gently removing her bent hands.

Shen asked his father if the money for signing over the claim on the family house had come through. Professor Shen nodded. It had been paid over to Fuming's creditors. His brother was out of jail and back in business.

"Can I borrow against the business?" asked Shen. He told

his father about Ruth's illness.

Money found, money spent, money paid, money borrowed. Where did it end? The old professor raised his eyebrows. "So you want money for your girlfriend's operation? Has she no people of her own? Let her get money from overseas."

"There's no time," Shen said.

"You should not have quit your job," his father reprimanded. "You should have foreseen this."

"How could I foresee this, Father?"

"You have valuable objects you can sell."

"There's nothing left, Father." Shen paused, always a collector, proud of his finds, as his father was always the inquisitive historian. "Only this," he went on, delving into the backpack.

"Old paper," his father sniffed, looking at the stitching and the thick black print.

"The lost chapters of an old book. Chapter Five and Chapter Six of *Six Chapters of a Floating Life* by Shen Fu. Qing dynasty."

The old man was unable to keep his fingers off. A sense of delight had bubbled up from deep inside him, rippling the surface of his stern face: a child's joy–like a feather brushing the back of his neck. "I know that book," he said. "Remember how I used to talk to you about it when you were a boy. Yun–and Shen Fu. How idle and absurd their life was. Froth and bubble. Oh, I used to love that book."

Shen was surprised. He did not remember his father ever mentioning the book.

"I remember," said his mother, stroking Shen's arm. "Your father was full of enthusiasms when he was young."

"Four out of six, that's all there was. Then it just drifted away. The author had such a funny way of writing. The ending was engraved on my mind. I still have it with me. The revolution has not swept that nonsense away.

From that time on I was again thrown into life's mad turmoil, a floating dream from which I do not know when I shall wake up!

"That's *not* the end, Father," said Shen. "I have found the true ending, and it has cost me dear. Now I have not a penny to my name to pay for my Ruth's medical treatment, who is as dear to me as Yun was to Shen Fu. I have only debts and burdens. I beg you to help me."

On Ruth's account Shen was willing to abase himself before his father in the traditional way.

Professor Shen's hands were shaking with excitement as he held the two chapters in anticipation of reading the text, finishing the book of his youth after so long a deferment. "Leave this stuff with me," Professor Shen said, "and I'll see what I can come up with."

"Have they demolished the house already?" young Shen blurted.

"The wrecking company ran into some problems with the water company that owns the pipes under the house. There's a stalemate for the time being. It's still standing, but part of the walls are down. They told me you left some things there. I'm supposed to fetch them or they'll take them for themselves.

The whole city's turning into a rubbish dump for looters and scavengers. That's what the revolution has done for us."

Shen did not want to hear his father's bitter, disillusioned words. Like a child who has been scolded, then forgiven, tears of gratitude came to his eyes simply at the thought that his father might find him some money.

"When your foreign girlfriend's better," advised the old man as he saw his son to the door, "send her back home and find someone else who can give me a grandson. You'll do better with one of your own kind. One of us. No one does any good from a sickly wife."

❋ ❋ Ruth lay under the sheet with her eyes closed, turned away from the sunlight that came through the open blind in an affront. After Dr. Jiang left, the nurse who was her friend brought another mug of black brew for her to drink. It took patience, the nurse said, to achieve true healing. She was from the countryside and, despite all her training in modern scientific methods, her deepest faith lay in the old remedies. She understood the power of conviction and clucked with approval at the weird array of ingredients in the prescription Ruth had brought with her from Tianzhou. Humble things, rare things, and their bitter fumes. She made sure Ruth drank the stuff four times a day. Ruth scratched the purple spots on her skin. Absurd and futile seemed to be the actions she had taken against her fate.

Then Ruth opened her eyes and saw Han.

Han strode into the room without knocking, her heels

clicking, her legs scissoring. Ruth rolled over, lifting her body against the bed pillows, and slowly opened both eyes. Han was in black from head to foot. She took off her dark glasses and folded them away into her pocket, allowing Ruth to see her piggy red eyes.

"Where have you been?" Ruth asked.

"Oh, here and there. Busying myself to death."

"Can I see your ring?"

Han stepped forward and held out her hand. Ruth examined it clinically. The diamond was something to be admired. Next to it was a thick gold band. The jade bracelet was on the opposite arm.

"You can touch it if you like," Han said. "Are you surprised to see me? I came as soon as I found out you were here."

The beauty has fallen into the hands of the barbarian.

"The barbarian has finished with this beauty for the time being," laughed Han.

Ruth patted the bed and Han sat beside her.

"What's the matter with you?" asked Han.

"I'll probably die in here," said Ruth flatly.

Han screwed up her face. Ruth was jinxing herself to talk like that.

"The best cure for my blood disorder is to remove my spleen. Spleen, you know? An irrelevant part of the body. It doesn't make sense. I don't want them to cut me open. It will kill me."

"Then don't."

"They say I'm incurable otherwise."

"Can you stall for time?"

"That's what I've been doing."

"What if they can't find you to operate? I mean, you should get out of here."

"They won't let me go."

"How can they stop you? I can fix it."

"I can't even walk," protested Ruth.

She was aware of Han's excited breathing, her breasts rising and falling. Han leaned forward and took hold of Ruth's shoulders. Ruth felt the energy run up her spine. "I'm getting you out of here," insisted Han.

Han went to the desk and chatted with the nurse. The nurse said no patient left the hospital without the doctor's permission. Han asked what happened if the doctor was unavailable. The nurse said that the floor superintendent could sign for the doctor and added that if the foreign girl was feeling well enough to go, it was thanks to the herbal medicine.

"Help us out, won't you?" asked Han.

The nurse hesitated for a moment, then said she could get the form signed later. She went with Han to Ruth's bedside and unhooked the intravenous drip. Ruth felt dizzy when she stood up and put on her clothes. The nurse gave Ruth a last jar of the herbal medicine to take with her, Han pressed some money into the willing nurse's hands and together they walked Ruth out of the hospital.

"Come back when you're ready," said the nurse, waving as the yellow taxi disappeared into the traffic.

"I want to see Shen's old attic," said Ruth. "I want to lie on that old bed."

"It's been demolished," said Han. "Don't you remember?"

"I want to see," said Ruth.

Through the tinted glass of the taxi Han turned her face to the noisy traffic and hard, close-packed buildings, the voracious life of the city, appreciating the risk they were taking. If an operation would kill Ruth, then so might this fantasy of escape. Realizing suddenly that she had been manipulated, Han feared what she was doing.

The taxi drove under the overpass into the old quarter where block after block had been flattened for the construction of the new freeway. But the house where Shen had lived, shorn of its neighbors and the wall around the perimeter, was still standing. Its bare brick and powdery mortar were exposed to the construction machinery that lay in wait in the yard. The windows were boarded over and looters had broken in, ripping out the art nouveau decoration. Itinerants had bedded down on newspapers and rags in the foyer, leaving a smell of urine. The house was an empty shell.

Ruth could barely make it up the four flights of stairs. Han cajoled and tugged at her. They rested on each landing. On the last Ruth sat down and would not get up until Han hauled her to her feet. When they reached Shen's door and found it padlocked, Ruth swore.

Han took out a tiny penknife and picked at the lock in vain. Then she went back down into the yard and found an iron pole, an old fence railing, to use as a crowbar. She split the old timber and the lock came asunder. They were inside.

The room had a pale coating of dust. The bed, dismantled, was still stacked in one corner as they had left it, with the trunk that contained Shen's personal things, his washing bowl, his kettle. The gas stove was still connected to the cylinder and enough water came out of the pipes to boil the kettle for tea. Ruth knew that if she bruised herself, her internal bleeding would never stop. But when Han needed help assembling the bed, Ruth helped her, oblivious of exhaustion, and together they managed.

With the bed erected, the room started looking like the place they remembered. They lay beside each other on the bed, sipping tea from broken cups, like elegant ladies, until Han started coughing from the dust.

"I'm going to give this place a good clean," she said, "while you sleep."

Soon the place had become quite homey. The rosewood posts of the bed frame glowed in the light of the four candles that Han had placed around it. The medicine pot simmered on the gas ring, its peculiar odors fumigating the place. Han sat on the polished chest, legs crossed, smoking a cigarillo, and Ruth slept. Her hair was like wisps of fire, her face still and calm. If this was death, thought Han coolly, it was not so bad.

But it was not death. Ruth's breath rustled her loose white shirt. A flicker of movement, alert, unconscious, played over her face as she stirred. She opened her eyes to Han and sat up, a sluggish energy entering her body. Slowly, easily, instinctively, she stood up.

"I feel better," she said.

Han puffed on her cigarillo. Ruth crossed the room and put a hand on Han's shoulder to steady herself. Looking away, Han inhaled the last of her cigarillo and stubbed it out. She stood there and let Ruth hug her. As they closed their eyes, the world was swimming with red for both of them.

"I'm so grateful," said Ruth.

"Don't overdo it," said Han. "You should eat something. I'll go out and get some food. You lie down."

"I'm not hungry."

"You must eat. Get your appetite back." Han tensed her mouth, humming.

"When can I hear you sing karaoke again?" Ruth asked.

"I'm through with that," said Han. "I'm making a CD."

Ruth grinned. "I finished my embroidery in hospital. Where is it? Where's my bag? It's for you."

Ruth rummaged in her bag and found the square of dark brown silk on which she had stitched the neat rows of gold Chinese characters. At the top was a golden lotus.

"Form is emptiness," she said, presenting it to Han, *"emptiness is form."*

Han rubbed the fine rough silk against her face. "I'll sleep on it," she said. "I don't have anything to give you in return. Sorry."

"You're here," said Ruth.

"This is originally yours," Han said, "and I return it to you. Full circle." With that she slipped her fingers from the jade bracelet and reached for Ruth's hand.

"It's yours, not mine," insisted Ruth. "Rightfully yours. I wanted it for you from the first moment I saw it. When I accepted it from Shen, I planned to pass it on to you. I asked Shen to give it to you. I had to find a way of making you accept it." Ruth spread her fingers so the bracelet would not go on. "The circle is *you*."

Han resisted. She wanted no more circles. Instead she wanted release. The love that had originated in their hearts and encircled them all must return to its source, traveling back along the red thread to its end. They took hold of the bracelet, both pushing it away, like a key on a string, laughing as each tried to force it over the fingers of the other, fingers splayed wide like an opening flower. They felt each other's breath, and the sweaty sheen of skin. Their eyes flashed. Head, neck, and shoulders angled and twisted. Their breasts brushed as their hands parried. Then the jade cracked, and instead of a circle there were two equal broken Cs.

In that moment the tension dropped from Han's body. She held the useless half-circle in a limp hand. Ruth laughed nervously, holding her half-circle up to one eye as if it were a monocle and glowering through it.

"Half each?" they said simultaneously, as if they were accomplices in a crime.

Ruth bit her lip. She felt faint again.

Han wrapped her half of the jade in the Heart Sutra cloth and put it in her bag. She tucked Ruth under the quilt, bent over her, and stroked her head. She was like a stray cat who had found a temporary home. Without opening her eyes, Ruth found Han's hand and squeezed it.

"It's a deal," whispered Ruth.

"I'll get some food," Han suggested guiltily. Then she was gone.

✻ ✻ After New Year I was asked by three friends to go and see the sing-song girls on the river. We went down in little boats that looked like eggshells cut in two. First we came to Shamian Island, where the flower boats were anchored in two parallel rows with a clear space in the center for smaller craft to pass up and down. We heard a confusion of footsteps as the girls came out. "Welcome, guests!" someone cried. I beckoned to one and she came forward with a smiling face and offered me betel nut. I put it in my mouth and, finding it harsh and unpalatable, spat it out. After cleaning my lips with a piece of paper, I saw I was besmeared with red like blood.

"People say that one should not come here in one's youth for fear of being enticed by sing-song girls," I said. "But when I look at these girls with their uncouth dresses and their barbarian dialect, I don't see where's the danger."

"You know there are Yangzhou sing-song girls across the river," said Chitang. "I'm sure if you go, you will find someone to your liking. The brothel keeper, Widow Shao, keeps only girls who really come from Yangzhou."

So we went across. The girls, some in red jackets and green trousers, others in green jackets and red trousers, some barefooted and wearing silver bracelets on their ankles, were lightly powdered and rouged and spoke a dialect we could understand. The so-called Widow Shao was a fat woman. Her hair was done up in a high coiffure by being wound around a hollow rack of silver wires more than four inches high. One of her temples was decorated with a flower held there by means of a long pin. She wore a black jacket and long black trousers that came down to the instep of the foot, set in contrasting sashes of green and red tied round her waist. She wore slippers without stockings and looked like someone in a circus. When we came onboard her boat, she bowed us in with a smile, lifting the curtain for us to enter the cabin. She was very cordial, but ugly to look at. She asked me to choose a girl.

I chose a very young one, who had short socks and embroidered butterfly shoes on her very small feet. Her figure was similar to Yun's. We let the boat anchor in the middle of the river and had a wine feast lasting until about nine o'clock. I was afraid that I might not be able to control myself and insisted on going home, but the city gate had been locked up at sundown in accordance with the custom of coastal cities, of which I was informed then for the first time.

By the end of the dinner, my friends were lying on the cushions smoking opium and fooling around with the girls. The attendants began to bring in bedding and were going to make the beds for all of us in the same cabin. I went to investigate the cabin on top of another boat, which was unoccupied. Widow Shao said, "I knew that our honorable guest was coming tonight and have purposely reserved this cabin for you." She led the way with a candle up the ladder at the stern and came to the cabin, which was compact like a garret. There was a bed and a small square window. "You can get a beautiful view of the moon from up on top," she said.

When Widow Shao left us alone, the girl and I crawled out through the window onto the top of the stern. A full moon was shining from a clear sky on the wide expanse of water. Wine boats were lying here and there like floating leaves. Their lights dotted the water surface like stars in the firmament. Through this picture, small sampans were threading their way and the music of string instruments and song was mixed with the distant rumble of the waves. I felt quite moved and thought to myself, This is the reason why one shouldn't come here in one's youth.

When I turned around and looked at the girl, I saw that her face resembled Yun's under the hazy moonlight, and I escorted her back to the cabin, put out the light and we went to bed.

The next morning Widow Shao appeared at the cabin very early. The girl had already slipped away. It was only then in the daylight I realized that Widow Shao was Han. This freakish round-faced woman, stout and ungainly, was what the singing girl had become. Han had recognized me at once and arranged for her new Yun to accompany me that night. The girl to whom she was most devoted.

I was uncertain whether to acknowledge her. I felt she might be embarrassed by her fate, although she seemed hearty and happy enough. Perhaps she preferred it to be her secret, that she could know who I was without suspecting that I knew who she was. In the last sharp gaze we gave each other, however, after I expressed my profound gratitude to her, I believe that everything between us was known.

Shen reached the hospital and went straight to the hematology department, but the faces in the corridor were all unfamiliar. The former patients had moved on already and new ones had taken their places, waiting their turns for treatment. The door of Ruth's room was ajar and the blinds were down. A dim gray light filled the interior, a cool sanitary silence. The bed, smoothly made, had not been touched. Only the lamp and a digital clock remained on the bedside table. It was Ruth's room no longer. Shen knew he had not made a mistake. Stripped of her possessions, the room was entirely impersonal, shadowy, and hygienic, as it had been when he and Ruth first arrived, in the cold state that patients usually did not see.

Where had she gone? To the operating room? To another floor? What if . . . ? Shen felt a layer of ice freeze around him. Could it happen so quickly? Life, death, and cleaning up afterward. At that moment her body might be lying . . . where? She had disappeared.

He rushed back down the corridor looking for someone he recognized. The unfamiliar nurses offered no information. Then just as he was beginning to panic, the nurse who had helped Ruth brew her herbal medicine came along, yawning after her tea break.

"What happened?" Shen asked desperately.

The nurse shrugged. "She checked out."

"When?"

"Just now. Her friend came and made the arrangements. She came and got her herbs."

"Her friend? Did she leave any message?"

"She was still quite frail," the nurse said. "I don't know if it was a good idea for them to go. But she wouldn't listen. I made her drink some more of that medicine to give her strength and I helped them get a taxi."

"Does the doctor know?" asked Shen.

The nurse was silent, dropping one shoulder a little.

"Thank you," he said, judging that the nurse had departed from standard hospital practice in this case. "Who was her friend?"

"A woman. A young miss. With money."

The old stairs creaked under his feet as he climbed. He had looked everywhere else for Ruth and Han before he remembered how Yun's spirit had returned to the room where she and Shen Fu found bliss, hiding in the flare of candles. When he pushed open the door, there was the bed with its blood-red sheen, four candles almost burnt away at each of the corners. In the draft from the door one of the candle flames sputtered and went out. There was Ruth, lying under the quilt. Through the dusty window and the wood lattice the dusk light was cast like a glowing cage. The room was ghostly, with still a fine powdery coating over everything, except the polished wood of the bed and his old camphor trunk.

"Han?" she murmured.

She was alone and there was no sign of how she had got there or what state she was in. He hesitated to stir her.

"No," he said. "It's Shen."

"Shen," she repeated with pleasure in her voice. She opened her eyes and looked at him as he came over. He sat beside her. She was solid warm flesh beneath the quilt. "I escaped," she said. "I wanted to come here. I'm waiting for the building to collapse around me." She smiled, her face full of light and movement, her skin lucent. A film had been removed from her eyes, a heavy, inert layer. "I don't need the operation, Shen."

"What has cured you?" he asked, humoring her. Certainly she looked quite different.

"Dr. Feng's medicine."

His eyes roved over her. He was skeptical, but there was no doubting the pulse of vitality he saw in her, wherever it came from. "Has Han come back?" he asked.

"She rescued me from hospital," Ruth said.

"Where is she?"

"She's gone to get something to eat," Ruth replied.

"I can't believe the change in you," Shen said, running his hand over her warm cheek. "It's just as the missing chapters say, that Han will redeem herself in another life and my Yun will be saved."

"You were right about the book all along," Ruth said. "We have waited all this time."

"Two hundred years," laughed Shen. His spirit was so light. He began to kiss Ruth. "I would have been like a dried stick burnt to gray ash without you. No life, just roaming aimlessly in search of the past. Now we have a chance." He was almost climbing into bed with her.

Just then a second candle guttered out. "I'd like to go back to that little town . . . to the inn," she said.

"Where all our troubles started?" he moaned.

"My prescription has nearly run out. I need to see Dr. Feng again."

"Ruth, your father is coming–and your stepmother. They're on their way to Shanghai," he said eagerly. "Just as you wanted it. They'll be here tomorrow morning."

She put her hand across her mouth, shaken by the reminder of her life. She saw her father's broad face, his receding hair, his forehead like the moon. Was it still black, his sleek, thin hair? His bristling black moustache used to be flecked russet and white, and a sparkle of hope was always in his eyes. Hope, disappointment, endlessly renewing hope. She repeated the information to herself. "He's actually coming here? For the last rites."

"No, for the operation," Shen said.

Ruth giggled. "Well, he'll get a surprise, won't he? Is he really coming? That's so sweet. But he doesn't need to come now. We'll have to stop them."

They heard the sound of someone's footsteps climbing the stairs of the empty house, the boards groaning, the cavernous spaces resounding.

"That'll be Han," said Ruth.

Shen went out onto the landing to investigate. It did not sound like Han's brisk tread. The beam of a flashlight slanted up the stairwell as the steps approached.

"Who is it?" Shen called.

"Fuling! Is it you, son?" his father's low voice responded. Professor Shen's shadow loomed on the wall as the old man came around the turn of the stairs and paused for breath. In the dim light his features were stark. "The demolition people called me and said there were intruders in the attic of the house. They were too scared to go in. Frightened it might be hooligans–or a ghost. Are you alone?"

Shen led the way into the room. His father followed like a mole, and again the draft from the door blew out a candle, leaving only one burning. In that thick, faint light he saw the young woman, her fair hair, her golden skin, her loose white shirt glowing eerily in the gloom. He pointed the flashlight beam in her face, making her look bloodless.

"So it's you." Professor Shen laughed dryly. "The little fox. Well, you can't stay here. All the obstacles are out of the way now. They continue the demolition tomorrow. Early." He spoke in an academic tone, savoring the irony of permanence and impermanence. "This house is as good as gone. It's history."

"Your father's house," Shen observed quietly.

"Don't remind me," his father chided. "That landlord father of mine brought me enough trouble with his grand dream of a house that no one could ignore. Yes, it's all history now."

Shen ignored his father's mordant reaction. "Ruth is recovering, father. She's on the mend. The sickness that threatened her life has receded as a direct consequence of finding those missing chapters of Shen Fu's book."

"Don't be a fool," his father said.

"Did you read Chapter Five, where the Buddhist master says that Han will have another chance in another life to return to Yun, and that Yun's illness will be cured as a result so they can happily continue their floating life?"

Professor Shen snorted. He pulled Chapter Five, rolled up, from his coat pocket. "For someone employed as an expert at an auction company, you are woefully ignorant, my son. The thing's obviously a fake." He slapped it down on the bed and opened it up, using his pen light to point at a passage. "That way of writing, those characters, don't you know? They're early twentieth century, Republican period. Part of the reform of the literary language. The real Shen Fu could never have used words in that way."

Professor Shen wielded the beam of light like a scalpel from word to word, pointing out modern simplifications of Chinese characters, newly invented forms, changes in usage– few and far between, but enough to give the game away. "It's a most diverting forgery, concocted in the old-fashioned style of Shen Fu's time by a scribe who wanted to please lovers of the book by letting them indulge their ideas of how the story might end. It's a decadent piece of work without historical roots or context," pronounced the old cadre, the dialectical materialist. "You've been willfully blinded, my son, by what you wanted to believe."

But the content of the chapters had already been proven authentic, on the pulse of life itself. Han's return and Ruth's health were flesh-and-blood testimony to the truth of what was written. His father may be telling him on the basis of some pedantic chronology that none of this could be so. Yet Shen was living the story in actuality, as his own.

"There should be laws against this sort of thing" the old man proclaimed. "Our country is developing. The regulations are not in place. You can have it back," he said, handing over the pages for which Shen had paid so dearly. "And I'm sorry, son, you can't stay here. This place is off-limits now. It's a danger zone. It no longer has anything to do with us. For your own safety and hers, you better leave at once." He screwed up his face, making the lines of a lifetime into a map of the knotted complexities of human ways and means. "You can go to your brother's place. He's back at his home now. He knows you gave up your place for him. Well, I won't hold you up."

After Professor Shen left, young Shen placed the copies of Chapter Five and Chapter Six together with the rest of the book. Then he separated them.

"The bastard," he said. He pictured the gap-toothed dealer soaked in fragrant sweat in the Hangzhou sauna. If what his father said was true, they were victims of a cruel and elaborate trick, deceived by their own hopes. Shen had paid for the missing chapters with his pair of Chenghua stem-cups. But if the genuineness of the chapters was ever disproved, Situ had promised to hand the porcelain back.

"Han *has* come back to us," said Ruth.

They sat down beside each other on the bed where the last candle was disappearing into the pool of its own wax. Shen felt something hard on the pillow. He picked it up and felt its rough, broken ends. He held it up in the frail candlelight, a hook of jade, a crescent moon. "What happened?" he asked.

"It was an accident," she said. "Han and I were squabbling over it and it split right down the middle."

"It's worthless now," he said. But the jade retained its warmth.

"It is two separate halves now," she explained. Shen knew she was referring to Han.

Shen and Ruth slept there in the old Ming bed that night, in each other's arms, and Han did not come.

✷ ✷ The demolition gang started early. The area around the house was cordoned off and the foreman checked each room for vagrants. Ruth helped Shen pack the bed, but she felt faint and sat on the stairs to rest. Shen lugged the bed and the trunk and his remaining possessions down to the street, then he called Ricky, who came with the company van.

They stood across the road at a distance and watched as the wrecker's ball swung from the crane's end and crashed through the attic window, smashing glass and the lattice into matchsticks. It swung back on its chain and hit the wall again, causing bricks to belly, roof tiles to slide to the ground, and puffs of mortar to rise like smoke in the morning air.

As the huge iron ball bashed away at the building, holes appeared in the walls. Finally the roof collapsed to the ground, as neatly as a tossed pancake settling back into the pan. The rest of the building shimmied, one bit gave this way, another bit gave that way, in its own rhythm of collapse. Solid brick, timber, and concrete became a four-story cloud of dust, rumbling, groaning, thudding, powdery red in the early sun.

Shen felt each blow as a body wound. Ruth stood beside him, her eyes caked with dust. When she squeezed his hand, her flesh and blood felt more solid to him than the great old building now was. The top story was gone, his dwelling place, the attic where the family had retreated during eras of political vengeance, his beloved studio gone in the dull fury of a wrecker's ball. He would not have been able to stand there were it not for her.

There were no neighbors left, only passersby to enjoy the show. The pile of bricks and rubble rose higher as the lower floors caved in. Clumsily the ball attacked the last walls, knocking them to the ground before the bulldozers moved in.

All was gone, as quickly as that.

Shen thanked the foreman as a man might thank his executioner. He felt that someone had to speak for the originators of the house. The people who had built it and the people who had worked there were gone too. The thinning drift of dust down the street might have been the last exit of all their ghosts, blown into oblivion, now the house of generations was no more.

Leaving the roar of earth-moving equipment behind them, they drove in the cream-colored van to Ricky's apartment, where they could wash the dust off themselves.

"We've set the date for the next auction," said Ricky, falling into a chair opposite Shen. "It's next month. Those paintings from Zhang Jun are going in. You won't approve of the catalog entries, I'm afraid."

Shen looked at Ricky. It all seemed very far away.

Ruth stood under the shower for a long time, cleansing her skin and rinsing her hair. She was shaken by what she had seen. She rubbed the purple markings on her hands. She realized an iron ball was assaulting her too, willing the demolition of her spirit. She knew she must conserve her energy to withstand its next assault.

She emerged from the shower fresh and in clean clothes, but it was only the most precarious imitation of health.

Ricky smiled at her. "So," he went on, "whatever happened to Han? Have you guys been having a good time?"

❋ ❋ Shen took the train to Hangzhou, carrying with him the fake missing chapters and a volume of the *Ocean of Words*. The great historical dictionary of the Chinese language was as big as a pillow and as heavy as bronze. Shen understood now that the dealer's arrangement to meet him late at night in the sauna had been a ruse to hide his tracks. He contacted Old Weng for a lead on how he might find Situ again. Old Weng told him to be careful. But Shen was calmly determined. He was ready to demand that Situ return the wine cups, the precious Chenghua stem-cups with which he and Ruth had sealed their love.

The dealer lived in a new apartment building in a development area on the tea slopes outside the city. The address was a plain concrete high-rise. The power happened to be off and Shen had to trudge up countless flights of rough-cast stairs, lugging his fat dictionary. The door to Situ's apartment was fortified with bolts and locks. Shen pounded at intervals, but no one answered. Then he sat on the stairs and waited, not making a sound. After a long interval he heard a shuffling inside. Keys turned, bolts were drawn open, a crack appeared in the door. Shen saw the dealer's eyes peering out. The rogue had no choice. Situ opened the door and in a surly swing of his head he ushered Shen inside.

Situ locked the door again and crossed the room in front of Shen, slapping the floor with his thongs.

Shen did not touch the tea Situ brought him, but proceeded to give a lecture on the dates of changing forms and usage in written Chinese. He spoke zealously, with a cold pallor to his face that betrayed no emotion. His father had instructed him well.

The fat dealer sat opposite him in shorts and a singlet, looking like a healthy slug. He sucked up Shen's words, his cheeks puffing. "Interesting, interesting," he said at intervals, not disputing Shen's account as it moved closer to the characters used in the so-called fifth and sixth chapters. "Well, that puts a different complexion on things. New information. How everything changes. Always things we don't expect."

Shen kept his spine erect. "This proves that the material you gave me is not authentic. Our arrangement was that the deal is off if those chapters turn out not to be the real thing."

"That's right," said Situ with a slur. "But things have changed."

"Things *have* changed," repeated Shen. "That's right. So you will return the pair of stem-cups."

"I would of course"–the dealer spoke slowly–"according to our agreement, but they have moved on too."

"What do you mean? They are absolutely genuine." Now Shen's agitation showed.

"Oh, they're genuine," beamed the man, "which is why they have already gone to someone else. I could not hold on to them forever while scholars pored over those two chapters in an attempt to discredit them. Time was never specified in our arrangement."

Shen's neck cramped with tension. "But the stem-cups? You know who has them? You can get them back."

"I don't think it's as easy as that. What if that party has already let them go to someone else? And so on and so on. Such perpetual motion is hard to stop."

"You're a cheat," Shen spat. "Tell me who has them. I'll go to them and explain the situation. I'll beg them to do the honorable thing."

"I fear it would cost you a pretty sum of money to acquire those wine cups again. In any case, they have gone on their way in circumstances of the utmost discretion. My reputation would be at stake if I divulged anything of their whereabouts. Well, that's that, I'm afraid," said Situ, folding his arms. "I'm glad you came here today. I appreciate the research you have done on the language of the *Six Chapters*. I knew nothing of that. Scholarship is always making revisionary discoveries. You're welcome to hang on to them, of course, since they're yours, or now that you've read them, you can return them to me, if you like."

Shen flicked the fake chapters across the table in the dealer's direction. The browned folds of paper might have been dung as far as he was concerned. They deserved to stick to the charlatan who had managed to turn them into gold. Shen had, in any case, already taken the precaution of making a copy. He owed Situ no favors. Without further courtesies he stuffed the weight of the *Ocean of Words,* volume one, into his pack and demanded that Situ unlock the door.

He marched down the hill through the terraces of tea bushes that glistened in the misty sunshine until he found a bus stop. He had been cheated, robbed, emptied, divested and there was nothing he could do about it. He felt like the husk of a seed on the breeze. And still he did not know how Shen Fu and Yun's true story ended.

As the train rolled back to Shanghai, Shen thought of Ruth and forgot his anger, his disappointment, and his emptiness. He thought of the way she cherished little things, how she paused over what had been thrown aside, how she went out of her way to appreciate objects that were worn and tired. Her demands for herself were so modest, yet she gave with boundless generosity to those who were open to receive. Which was why Han's rejection had so devastated her. She never asked for Han's attachment, but when Han gave, she gave naturally in return. Then Han blocked off her capacity to receive. That was not something for which Ruth should have had to suffer. Ruth was steadfast. Her commitment was so pure. That was the quality he loved from the first moment.

6.

BEAUTIFUL GLEANINGS

Yun had a peculiar fondness for old books and broken slips of painting. Whenever she saw odd volumes of books, she would try to sort them out, arrange them in order, and have them rebound properly. When she saw scrolls of calligraphy or painting that were partly torn, she would find some old paper and paste them together nicely, and ask me to fill up the broken spaces. Then she would roll them up and label them "Beautiful Gleanings." This was what she was busy about the whole day when she was not attending to the kitchen or needlework. When she found in old trunks of musty volumes any writing or painting that pleased her, she felt as if she had discovered some precious relic. An old woman neighbor of ours used to buy up old scraps and sell them to her. Yun had the same tastes and habits as myself, and besides had the talent of reading my wishes by a mere glance or movement of the eyebrow, doing things without being told and doing them to my perfect satisfaction.

Once I said to her, "It is a pity that you were born a woman. If you were a man, we could travel together and visit all the great mountains and the famous places throughout the country."

"Oh, this is not so very difficult," said Yun. "Wait till my hair has gone gray. Even if I cannot accompany you to the Five Sacred Mountains, then we can travel to the nearer places, as far south as the West Lake and as far north as Yangzhou."

"Of course this is all right," I said, "except that I am afraid when you are gray-haired, you will be too old to travel."

"If I can't do it in this life," she replied, "then I shall do it in the next."

Shen and Ruth traveled to Tianzhou by boat that same night, arriving late and waking Mrs. Ma from her sleep. She was pleased to see Ruth looking so well.

First thing in the morning they went to find Dr. Feng, who was half expecting them. She knew that the prescription would have run out by now. If Ruth did not come, it would have been a bad sign. But after examining her, Dr. Feng was more than satisfied with her progress. The transformation was remarkable, but the treatment must continue she said, busily writing out another prescription.

Ruth was grateful to this skilled doctor for showing her that a remedy was available if ever again an emotional storm threatened to blow her off course. Dr. Feng beamed in contentment as she handed her patient the package of medicine. If you had time, the doctor said, you could always find a way. You must slowly stitch the body to the world that nourishes it, repairing the frayed threads of its own life principle. Saying this, she ran her fingers over the neat embroidery on Ruth's shirt, which Ruth had mended on the river.

They were saying their good-byes when Old Weng rushed in, breathless and shaking. Shen had never seen him so agitated. Hearing that the lovebirds had reached Tianzhou, he came rushing to find them, not allowing a moment's delay. He more or less dragged Shen and Ruth out of Dr. Feng's clinic and up the hill. Only when they were striding along like the wind did he think to congratulate Ruth on her return to health, but he made no concessions as he raced ahead up the cobbled road to the Yellow Corktree Temple.

At the entrance to the temple they stopped to look back at the town, as the young couple had done that first time, spread below like a soft, smoky quilt airing in the morning light, the waterways reflecting the sky. As they paused to catch their breath, Shen blurted out to Old Weng what had happened in Hangzhou. He had swapped his precious Ming dynasty stem-cups for the missing chapters of Shen Fu's book on the understanding that the deal would be reversed if they turned out to be phony. But when he tracked the man to his lair with proof, he was told that the stem-cups had already gone.

"Doesn't matter, doesn't matter," laughed Old Weng. "Dealer Situ always was a rogue. You got your fingers burnt.

But you had some interesting reading. Wait and see where it goes from here." He was rubbing his hands.

"In the end it goes back where it came from," Ruth said. "Even the finest porcelain is only baked clay, after all."

"It's the scarcity of survival that gives value," said Old Weng, rocking on his toes. "Come on, in we go."

They entered the main hall of the temple where an old monk was waiting. He had a birthmark on his cheek that looked like half of the Chinese character for *gate*. Old Weng introduced him as Broken Gate, the renowned head monk of the temple. He looked familiar to Ruth and Shen, although they had not met him on their previous visit. Overhead the giant face of the Buddha floated in gold among the blood-red beams of the temple roof as the candles danced and shafts of sun poked through doors and cracks. Oranges and waxy apples were piled up on the altar in offering, and incense twisted upward in wayward curlicues of smoke. This Sakyamuni Buddha sat cross-legged with downcast eyes and hands poised in the mudra of teaching. On either side of him were other statues, the avatars of destruction and rebirth. The stone floor clattered with the sound of people bobbing up and down in prostration. It was a busy place.

"You've come back," Broken Gate said, bowing inconsequentially. "This way, please."

Behind the main hall was a smaller hall dedicated to Guanyin, whose bright eyes seemed to follow the monk as he led them around the back and up the stone steps into the living quarters. When they reached a musty little reception room, he asked them to sit.

The head monk and Old Weng had been friends since boyhood. Their roads diverged years ago when Broken Gate took his vows and set off on his beggar's journey. But in the period of turmoil when the Yellow Corktree Temple was under threat, he returned to Tianzhou to protect it, like a son coming home to protect his parents, and Broken Gate and Old Weng resumed their old friendship.

"In those years, when all forms of religion fell under suspicion," Broken Gate said, "Yellow Corktree Temple was attacked time and again. Its funds were confiscated, its relics seized or smashed. Monks were denounced and pilloried, and many left the order, returning to secular life. At the lowest ebb, during the Great Leap Forward, the grand compound was designated a site for light industry. The commune members moved in and attempted to smelt iron here. It became a factory for producing electric fans. Only one small dormitory was set aside for the few remaining monks.

"At that time a humble and frail old man came to the temple. For many years he had lived his life as a hermit, and even now he drew no attention to himself. It was said that as he entered old age, according to the average life span of three score years and ten, he achieved enlightenment. Thereafter he made it his mission to save Buddhism in his native country."

Unhurriedly Broken Gate told the story. "Obscurely he went around from temple to temple carrying out the teaching with those who remained. The buildings were crumbling, rotting, being eaten by worms, and the monks and nuns endured deprivation and persecution without end. The master taught constantly so that the teachings would survive. By the time he reached our Yellow Corktree Temple, he was rumored to be more than one hundred and ten years old. One of the great living masters."

Broken Gate grinned as he remembered his old teacher.

"Enough prattling," said Old Weng. "Just get on with it. These young people haven't got all day."

"The master was subtle and canny," said Broken Gate. "He knew there were things that held no value or interest to those who were bent on a campaign of vindictiveness and greed. Treasures were looted or surrendered, but there were other poor things that might be passed over, or concealed without arousing suspicion if by chance they were discovered. Sutras, documents, meager relics. The old master was always careful not to implicate the other monks in what he did. They faced danger and adversity enough. He acted alone in what he did.

"Every so often he asked me to procure a new cash box for him. Assuming he had forgotten, I told him that I had already found him one. But he said no, that one had gone missing too. I wondered at the time why the cash box kept going missing. I had to go and pester my old friend Weng here, who worked in the records office of the security bureau at that time and had access to supplies of such things."

"That's when I learnt never to ask questions," Old Weng chuckled, hearing the story retold.

"It turned out that when the old master rose alone for meditation in the darkness before dawn, he was carefully removing the floorboards, digging down into the earth and burying the cash boxes, full of as many things as he could stuff into them. Cash boxes, to which he kept the keys.

"At last the authorities decided to close down our temple altogether," Broken Gate continued. "We had almost no warning. The master instructed us all to leave at once before ruffians stormed the place. I remonstrated with him, but he insisted that for the sake of the future of the teaching, *his* teaching, we must take off our robes and put on the blue cotton workers' uniform of those times and make our escape. Survive was what he ordered us to do. As for himself, he had decided to stay. He said if he was too old to remember his age, he was too old to run. He would look after things in his own way. No sooner had we left than a gang of thugs came and beat him to death at the entrance of the temple for all the world to see. Stinking Old Thing, they called him. Stinking Old Thing!"

Broken Gate wiped his eyes. "I returned as soon as I could," he said, "but it was many years before our life here was able to resume. Slowly we have been carrying out repairs, restoring the Yellow Corktree Temple to its old glory again. But all this time we have still not been able to rehabilitate the master's memory fully. That remains our prime task."

Shen shook his head, casting a quizzical glance at Ruth. They were both wondering why Old Weng had brought them there with such urgency to hear this old tale.

Fingering his beads, Broken Gate proceeded calmly. "We restored the compound stage by stage, starting with the main hall, leaving our living quarters to last. Last of all was that small dormitory at the back. It has such bad associations for us that no one wanted to sleep there, so it became the storeroom, where we keep our rice and oil. In the fall it became infested with rats that openly scurried in and out. As we Buddhists are not supposed to harm living creatures, we decided to have a good clean out and get rid of them that way. There were swallows nesting in there too, spiders and moths, and borers in the floorboards. Finally we set to work ripping up those rotten floorboards, and it was then, just the other day, that we heard a bent old nail fall to earth and hit something metallic. We dug down in that spot and found the master's cash boxes, twelve in all, buried in the ground under the floor. All this time they had been there and we never knew."

The old monk sat there in silence, enjoying the curiosity of his new listeners. He was an artful tale spinner. Shen and Ruth sat bolt upright with their senses alert for the denouement.

"The boxes were stuffed full of precious things," Broken Gate said. "Our scriptures. Commentaries on the sutras written by our patriarchs. Slips of paper, poems, a few paintings taken off their mounts. Relics of our Buddhist ancestors, including a little bamboo back scratcher in the shape of a hand that was said to be used by the poet Cold Mountain himself. Toothpicks, ear picks, and the master's own cloak of patched rags. Things for our museum," he grinned, "when we get it ready for the public. And finally this." He unrolled a bundle of paper, handling it with the utmost reverence. "The master's account of his own life."

Shen looked from Broken Gate to Old Weng for an elucidation of its contents. Why would the old men not simply explain? he asked himself. Why could they not go straight to the point? Or was this supposed to be enough, merely the end of another unrelated trail? While Shen disguised his quandary, the two old men watched eagerly for a reaction. But Shen dared not open his mouth.

"The master mentions his action in hiding the secret documents of the temple," Broken Gate went on. "He says there is something unusual among them that posterity might not expect to find there, if any of the documents were lucky enough to survive. It is the record of an exceptional incident that happened here, recollected by a literary gentleman toward the end of his life, that deserves to be added to the lore of the Yellow Corktree Temple. The true story of a woman brought back from the dead through the devotion of another. A testimonial to the compassionate power of Guanyin in relation to our earthly attachments. It was the author's stipulation that the story should not be published at the time, since he was not seeking worldly fame. The master's instructions are clear, however, that whatever survives among the buried documents is now ready to be published to the world. Have you guessed what I'm talking about? Here it is."

Broken Gate's smooth old hands laid out a gathering of sheets of handmade paper, each the size of a modern tabloid, on which were rows of characters written with brush and ink. Across the top in different calligraphy was inscribed: *The Continuation of the Life of Shen Fu—Two Chapters.*

Shen gasped. Then he giggled with childish excitement. Was it another hoax? It was almost beyond disbelief. Old

Weng stretched out his arms and grasped Shen and Ruth by their wrists. He did not need to say anything. His whole body was trembling over the find. Ruth felt it in his grip. He was passing on his conviction that here at last was the truth.

Broken Gate held out a pair of embroidered shoes, scarcely faded at all. "These were in the same box," he said.

Ruth looked at them and smiled. They were identical to the pair she had worn the night she met Shen, the pair she made herself.

"Yun must have had big feet for those days," she said.

"What's this?" Shen asked, noticing the frayed strip of cloth lying in the monk's hand.

"The pages were rolled up and the shoes were stuffed inside. It was all tied into a bundle with this bit of red," explained Broken Gate.

"What does the manuscript say?" asked Shen, looking at each of the old men in turn. "Have you read it?"

"The monks need money to carry on their work," said Old Weng. "They have decided to sell the manuscript to the highest bidder."

"Such a manuscript is beyond price," Shen said, "if it's genuine." He had still not worked out what the old collector was getting at.

"Oh, it's genuine," said Broken Gate. "We have the master's word for that. Mr. Shen, you have connections with the auction business. We would like you to handle this matter for us. Not everyone can be trusted with something like this, you see. Will you do it?"

Shen was about to burst. An auction was the last thing he had on his mind. He desperately wanted to know the contents of the missing chapters, now found. That was all he cared about. "I'm unworthy of this honor," he replied with stilted formality. Ruth laughed and gave him a little shove. Broken Gate had reaffirmed his vocation as a handler of old things. Shen could get his job back simply by turning up at Stanley Hummel's office with an item of the quality of this newly discovered manuscript. And if he wanted to find out what was in those two missing chapters, then he had to agree to do what Broken Gate asked. Ruth saw it all. That was the old monk's deal. Shen was to be responsible for taking the sole surviving original version of the missing chapters of Shen Fu's life to the market and the world.

Humbled by that trust, the young man shook Broken Gate's hand and tucked the precious manuscript under his arm. It took all his self-restraint not to peek. Ruth put her arm round him and kissed his cheek. She was happy. Shen had at last found what he was looking for. He wondered why she was so calm.

❋ ❋ Old Weng accompanied Shen and Ruth down the hill; when they reached his house he invited them in and his wife brought tea. He closed the shutters and turned on a lamp. The old paper could not be exposed to direct sunlight. It was yellowed around the edges as if soaked in weak tea and the rows of words continued on in a steady beat for sheet after sheet, with occasionally a correction or an insertion from the margin, like someone pacing out the unforeseen way of their life.

There in the safety of Old Weng's home they leafed through the pages of the manuscript while Old Weng summarized the contents.

"You see, the singing girl did come back to Yun. That much is true. Han escaped from her cruel husband and went looking for her friend, but she came too late. She found only the trappings of Yun's funeral and the monk's warning that she must return to this world of dust in a future life to make amends for betraying Yun's helpless devotion. It's just as the Hangzhou dealer's forgeries say. Perhaps their author had heard something, some hearsay passed down from mouth to mouth. The forgery may not have been completely without merit, young Shen. Those chapters, written according to the taste of a later time, are yours too, acquired at such cost. You must go back to Situ and reclaim them.

"But from that point on, the story goes quite a different way," said Old Weng. "The singing girl refused to leave the monks' company. She took upon herself the task of tending Yun's grave, which was part of the monks' duty. She changed her life to one of sacrifice, dedicating herself to the way of the Buddha. Day and night she made devotions to Guanyin, Goddess of Compassion, begging for Yun's life to be restored. Of course all this was quite unknown to Shen Fu. Perhaps it was an idle dream, or behavior of hysterical madness; nevertheless the monks found a place for Han and humored her. She shaved her hair, wore the humble robes of a nun, went barefoot, and ate her simple meals from a plain wooden bowl. She sang her songs for Yun's spirit to hear and at night she would shiver in bed, as if turned to ice, knowing that Yun's restless spirit would not leave her alone.

"The continuation of Shen Fu's account has lodged safely here at Yellow Corktree Temple all this time," said Old Weng. He bowed his head. He was weary, as if the task of his lifetime had been brought to completion by passing the responsibility over to young Shen. He was tired now and asked to be left alone. So they made their farewells.

On the way back to Shanghai, Shen and Ruth read the pages, the columns of lively and elegant calligraphy, poring over the words as they had on their first night together. Shen did not notice, as he peered at Shen Fu's wrinkled script, that Ruth was short of breath in the chilly air on the top deck of the boat.

She was a little dizzy, a little feverish. She felt like a dinghy that is tugged loose from its mooring by a nagging breeze and carried away, blown to an unknown destination on a distant shore.

I traveled the country as an assistant to my boss, carrying out petty administrative duties and all the time grieving for my lost wife and lamenting the vanished happiness of the past. Most of all I dreaded returning home where Yun should have been waiting for me, but in the end, my business done, I had no choice.

The day came when I walked through the gate into the courtyard of our old home. I was just about to enter the door of the house when Yun came out to greet me, just as a wife greets her husband, with kisses on my face and her hands on my chest, so I could feel at once that she was flesh and blood. This was no hallucination or ghost. But when I tried to ask her, she silenced me.

"I thought you were–" I queried, not daring to say the word. She protested that it had all been a misunderstanding. I knew I had sat beside Yun's corpse. I had crawled on my hands and knees in the mud over her grave. Was that all a dream? But I was so happy to have her back that I questioned no more.

So we lived on, just like an ordinary couple. I never asked her where she had been or how she had come back. She gave no indication that she was not the same as the other creatures of this world. I would travel, sometimes far and wide as I took different posts, and when I did so I always thought of my dear wife, sometimes seeing her in the beauties of nature, sometimes seeing her in the faces of other beauties I met–I have a roving eye and I confess I was not always faithful–but then I would return home and there she would be, warm and witty, with her things about her, live growing things and old decaying things, new discoveries, funny new ideas. Sometimes when no one was looking, we would go out together at sunset or by the light of the full moon–that was when Yun liked to disguise herself as a man to deflect attention–and visit temples and pavilions in places that overlooked the world.

For many years we lived passionately together in this manner, finding so many ways to express our love for each other, as if every moment was a gift, a joyous surprise snatched from borrowed time.

Then one day our excursions brought us here, to Tianzhou, to pay a visit to the famous Yellow Corktree Temple. By this time Han had moved away from the place where Yun's body had been buried. She had taken her nun's vows and lived in retreat from the world. For some time she lived in distant mountains, before returning to live obscurely as a temple servant, continuing her selfless devotion to the Goddess Mother Guanyin.

It was in the same hall where the image of Guanyin stands today that we saw the skinny barefoot nun robed in brown, her bowed head fuzzy as a peach, leaning on her straw broom as she swept the stones, her eyes downcast. She must have observed us from behind. On an impulse Yun turned, as if to brush away a mosquito that was buzzing around her neck, and in that moment she met Han's gaze. Han knew then that her faith had been answered. Quietly she looked down and resumed sweeping the floor. She needed no more than that instant of recognition.

That night Yun and I slept in the little inn by the temple gate. We made love, united as ever. I did not know it would be for the last time. In the morning, when I woke from sleep, she was gone.

I sought her through all the world after that, traveling in wider and wider orbits, the length and breadth of the land, but I never saw her again. Sometimes–often–I was tricked by an illusion. The happiness when Yun first returned was a secret between the two of us, so now I did not broadcast my grief in continuing on without her. It was private. I had no explanation for her sudden disappearance. I kept it all inside until, many years later, when I was revisiting the places where we had gone together, I came back to Tianzhou and the temple here.

The nun was gone, long gone, no one knew where, but before she left she had told her story, by way of confession, to her teacher. She told of her attachment to a young gentleman and his brilliant wife and their attachment to her beyond all bounds, and her betrayal of those feelings, which brought about the sudden death of the woman who loved her and broke the gentleman's heart. From that time on she had devoted herself to the Buddha's teachings in order to make amends. One day, here in this temple, she discovered that divine compassion had reunited the man and his wife as a loving couple in this world, the woman who also visited her at night in her dreams and made her freeze in the embrace of a body of ice.

As the eyes of the two women met in the hall that was devoted to Guanyin, where she used to sweep the stones, the missing element of heat returned to them both. It sparked between them a powerful current. The thread of restless craving that bound them was *still* unbroken. The Goddess Mother had honored that attachment too. But now the time was up. That same night the wife left her husband's bed and returned again to the spirit world.

The teller looked at me as he concluded his story. The same man had been Han's confessor. He looked at me and saw, perhaps, a weary middle-aged visitor, a seeming failure in this life. He asked idly if I had any response to his tale, probably wondering whether I believed it or not. I simply replied, "I am that man. I am Shen Fu."

It only remained for me to write down the record of my life. When I came to the latter part, however, I decided to keep it secret, as I had kept secret Yun's return for fear of ridicule and for fear of being accused of loving a ghost. I knew how real she was, how warm and flowing her blood.

I do not write this part of my life for the entertainment of my friends as I wrote about my early married life and my financial worries and my aesthetic theories and my travels and adventures. I write exclusively for the annals of the temple, my own partial account of a wonder brought about through the boundless compassion of the bodhisattva in defiance of death. Here in the temple my story will lodge.

The river, catching the lights of the moving clouds, was like a billowing length of gray silk. Boats plied back and forth, sometimes a bird whirled overhead, colors flashed here and there, on a billboard, a wall, a gold temple roof. Shen and Ruth sat like sacks of rice on the top deck, reading the manuscript. They ate ice cream. Ruth pointed out to Shen the withered lotus stalks, like broken umbrellas, in the mud ponds along the way. They were as serene as fisher-folk who have hauled in their catch.

The embroidered shoes were proof of a double destiny. And more than the knowledge they accumulated from the earlier lives of Shen Fu and Yun was the familiarity they felt with each other, the intimacy of feeling, the meaning of a glance, the touch of skin, the reverberation of presence with memory. In this they seemed to merge into one, so that Shen might feel sensations that Yun had felt and Ruth feel what Shen Fu had known. Such complexity could lead to confusion–it has done so, time and again–but here, as the riverboat chugged toward Shanghai, it was understood, it was entirely harmonious.

✷ ✷ We docked and trooped off the ferry with the other passengers. The precious manuscript was held tightly under my arm. We had nowhere to stay and it was already dark so we decided to take a pedicab through the back alleys to my old office in the hope of catching Ricky before he left work. He had remained a good friend to me through everything. My old Ming bed was in storage at his place and we hoped we could sleep there. I did not want to let the manuscript out of my sight, however, and I thought it better not to tell Ricky about it until after I had settled things with Stanley and the manuscript was locked away in the safe at Shanghai Art Auctions International.

If Stanley agreed to reinstate me and was willing, on this one rare item, to split the commission so I could repay my debts, and if he promised never again to ask me to compromise my connoisseurship, then I would be happy enough to go back to my old job and set my life on a steadier course.

"You look as though you're about ready to eat humble pie," quipped Ricky, assuming I would have to grovel to Stanley to get myself employed again. "That'll be something to see. How are you, darling?" He gave Ruth a kiss. "The gallery's been chasing you. A couple of your pictures are ready for collection. There's only one or two that didn't sell. They've got your money for you."

"Oh dear," Ruth sighed histrionically. "That'll be something else to store at your place, Ricky."

"I'll hang them in memory of you. In case you forget to come back."

"We're not going away again," I vowed to Ricky.

We were laughing as we left the building together. It was a pretty Shanghai night, lights shining purple, pink, and orange, people circulating on the lookout for something new to notice–a new demolition, a new façade, a new makeover, always something never tried before–launched with a supply of optimism, a craving for novelty, that was endlessly renewed.

We sallied out into the streets, three friends, and found a welcoming little place where we could eat some snacks. Over dinner Ricky told us about a fancy new club that had opened up, more stylish and refined than the Red Rose. Since Han left, he said, the Red Rose had gone right downhill.

Blue Skies, the new place was called. I was a little edgy about going there with my precious manuscript on my person, the true missing chapters, but I vowed to stay sober and keep it in my sight at all times. We drove there in a taxi and Ricky offered to treat us the admission. He was doing all right and had not yet found a lover to spend his money on.

The entrance to Blue Skies was a mock-up of the pearly gates, golden pillars, pink-and-white clouds, and bluebirds peeping all over. The place was full to the rafters and the bouncers were under strict orders to let no one in until there was a table vacant for them. We lingered on the steps, waiting, enjoying that special atmosphere of Shanghai, of preeminence and promise, that makes you want to be nowhere else. This was our city, our life, this was the future coming into being–that's how we felt.

The bouncer told us he would squeeze the three of us into a banquette for two that was just being vacated. He pointed at a spot on the far side of the room. Through the rays of a light show we could see a man helping a woman into her jacket as they prepared to leave. With Ricky leading the way, we headed across the floor in their direction.

The departing couple chose a different exit route through the crowded tables, so we did not pass close to them. I got a look at the man, though, a well-dressed, well-heeled Hong Kong type, block-shaped, cold-faced. The woman who came after him was a local. I couldn't see her face, only her boyish figure. I guessed she was the Hong Kong fellow's date for the night. Then she turned and caught sight of Ruth and burst into a delighted smile. It was Han.

She waved. She waved to us both, but her eyes were for Ruth. She gestured at Ruth to come over, rolling her eyes comically at her escort who was pulling her along by the hand. Ruth gave a smile of ineffable sweetness in return. But although she was drawn after Han, she held herself back. Tables and people were in the way, crowding the dark room, and Han was moving on, tugged by the man who would not let her go, and Ruth was caught between Ricky and me. It was impossible for her and Han to reach each other and speak.

Han blew Ruth a last kiss as she disappeared out the door. That was all.

Ruth was very quiet that night. She seemed to enjoy herself in a detached way. Ricky paid attention to me, courting me a little, overjoyed that I was coming back to the office. I was his mate, he said, looking at me with swooning eyes until Ruth pushed me off to dance with him. She whispered me a promise that she would guard the manuscript with her life.

I was relieved when at last we got safely back to Ricky's with the manuscript still in my possession, and I was very content to go to sleep with Ruth in my own bed.

Stanley received me cordially the next morning, but he was suspicious when I showed him the manuscript. He suspected me of plotting my revenge. He was incapable of making his own assessment, and even when Ricky vouched for my story he continued to be wary. He was a cautious man who doubted his own judgment. Linda was still unforgiving toward me too, and Stanley would have to deal with her at home. The risk of such an exceptional find going to his competitors should have been enough to sway him, however, along with my hard-won reputation for integrity. Finally he decided that if I was prepared to certify the manuscript's authenticity, he was willing to make a deal. He agreed to my terms–to split the auctioneer's commission with me and take me back on staff. I thanked him profusely.

Through my father's contacts I undertook to call scholarly experts to examine the manuscript. Really I had no doubts at all. The only question was the timing. Once word was out about the find, the news would spread like wildfire among those with a penchant for such things. So I donned my suit and tie and returned to work.

I'm not sure what Ruth did in those days. She drifted about the city and we met up again in the evenings. I treasure the memory of going out with her and of idling sweetly at home like an ordinary doting couple. I don't think Ruth saw Han again after that glimpse of her, when she left the nightclub in a hurry. I was worried that the sight of Han might stir up the murky currents of abandonment in Ruth and affect her health. But there were no signs of that.

I can see that Ruth was strange in those days. Not herself, as if already moving away, like a fading photograph. Behind her bubbling serenity she was distant and detached. She responded to my ardor with all her usual passion. When our bodies formed an intimate circle and we passed through that O to become one, there seemed to be no bounds to our bliss. Perhaps we had gone as far as our carnal love could go and there was still something else, some part of ourselves that was not implicated in it, and that perplexed us. I said to her that sometimes I felt as if Yun and Shen Fu were watching our lovemaking from either side of the bed and their separate gazes were gradually drawing us apart.

"Don't you see?" Ruth replied. She looked at me with her characteristic candor, her pale eyebrows raised, a spiky aura of hair, her skin translucent and her eyes offering me, with all their tenderness, the absolute clarity of what she saw. "It's all there in the book, as you always knew it would be, in Shen Fu's secret continuation of his story. Yun comes back from the dead because of Han's devotion and Shen Fu's love. Granting the power of those still unbroken attachments, the bodhisattva breaks the rules of life and death for a far longer time than humans dare to ask, and still the story is uncompleted. Still our love for each other brings us back again. Still the vital flow of feeling in Han's devotion brings us back to our earthly selves. Still we are bound. Why?" She held my hand. "What purpose does it serve? What does it ask of us? It's surely time to cut the thread. We don't lose by doing that. We only gain."

I found her words obscure. I worried that she was troubling herself with convoluted thoughts, spending too much time alone. We did not have a house of our own to go to, and we had not yet fully resumed a settled life. I was concerned that she might get sick again, but I didn't say anything because I didn't want to make her anxious. I leaned forward and put my arms around her in a long, tight hug. I could not see beyond her, desirable and rare, the only person I would ever love. When I speak of the sensation of complete sweetness I felt in that moment, I am confident I speak for her too. No amount of lifetimes can erase that from the record of experience.

"We met on the night of the Cowherd and the Weaving Girl," she said. "Do you remember? They come together once a year, when their separate stars are close enough for them to meet, and their story is repeated year in and year out. We're not like them. We have only one story, a long and complicated meeting through cycles of time and space. There's no one else like us."

I laughed, relieved, and hugged her again, confident that we would indeed disprove the adage and reach old age together as a loving couple.

✺ ✺ When the day of the auction came, people flew in from all over the world. The veteran auctioneer with the polka-dot bow tie was hired once again. Once more the ballroom of the former French club was filled with sensational flower arrangements and matching red-and-yellow banners. The rich, hopeful, shrewd, and curious thronged the place. The Deputy Mayor sat in the front row beside Linda, with Ivy and Zhang Jun. To Linda's great relief, Zhang had become an item with Ivy, although somewhere in the background was still the wife who had given him his start in life, busy presiding over the airport. Poor Ivy! I noticed that the Deputy Mayor had no catalog, as if the auction were nothing to do with him.

The first lots were terra-cotta figures with the dirt still on them brought in from the back blocks around the old capital of Chang'an. It looked as if the local tomb robbers had touched up the paint on them too. They were ancient but undistinguished and the market was glutted with such things by now. Their fate was to be decorator items in hotel lobbies and penthouse apartments. They broke no records.

Then came the Deputy Mayor's paintings. The auctioneer gave them a real rap. No doubt some people knew the provenance because there was a buzz in the room. Ricky had obliged Stanley with high claims and estimates for each of these works in the catalog. He kept out of the way, skulking behind the information desk at the back of the hall. Bids came in from those who were willing to curry favor with the Deputy Mayor on a gamble. The auctioneer whipped the public up. But the bids soon petered out. The Deputy Mayor stiffened angrily. Linda shuffled the pages of her catalog, looking round in vain for her husband as if there had been some mistake. The reception was cold, as if people knew the paintings were spurious.

Zhang bowed his head, knowing he would have to take the blame. Ivy was the color of a tomato. One by one the Deputy Mayor's paintings failed to come within reach of their absurd reserves and were withdrawn.

I stood in the wings with Stanley, not daring to look at him. No doubt he held me responsible for sabotaging his ambitions, when I had done nothing except have my eye vindicated. I tried not to show my glee.

The auction had taken an interesting turn. The lots moved on. There was good and bad, worthless and ordinary and special. It was up to the bidders to decide.

"Lot 26," announced the auctioneer, and here the hush fell. "We are proud to offer to you today, ladies and gentlemen, the author's original manuscript of the missing final section of Shen Fu's classic literary work *Six Chapters of a Floating Life*. The missing chapters, discovered after nearly two centuries, fully authenticated, have never been seen in public until now." The ballroom was silent with awe. Maybe there were some skeptics, but the majority belief in the manuscript's genuineness was palpable. "When you are ready, ladies and gentlemen. What am I bid?"

The bidding was an avalanche, coming from all sides, building on itself, implacable, unstoppable. Just short of two million dollars the auctioneer's hammer rose into the air, lingering, hovering, as he called for second and third thoughts before striking the gavel in a blow that made the room shake. The once-in-a-lifetime rarity went to an institution in Taiwan that was prepared to pay such a staggering amount for the custodianship of our Chinese heritage. I hugged myself in disbelief.

Twelve and a half percent of that money was mine. I ran out from the wings and shook the auctioneer's hand. I looked about the room. There was Old Weng, standing at the back. He closed his eyes sagely. It was as near as he would go to a wink. We had made a fortune for the Yellow Corktree Temple.

Then I looked around for Ruth. I scanned the room row by row, right to the back corner. I could see clearly how she stood there the first day I ever saw her; my gaze had gone straight to her and she had looked back at me, reading me, as I found out later, in my sudden impulse to withdraw *Six Chapters* from sale. She had been there a few moments ago, in the same place she had stood that first day. Yet now I could see her nowhere.

Ricky said she was a little overcome by the stuffiness and had stepped out for a breath of air. I thought I might find her sitting in the hotel grounds, but all the benches in the garden were empty. Other people were strolling along those paths. I guessed she must have gone back to Ricky's to rest, so I jumped into a taxi and went to find her. But she was not there either. I ran around town frantically checking every possible place. The Blue Skies, the hospital. I even asked a taxi to take me to my old house and only when I got there did I remember that the house was gone. Something new was already going up in its place. There was a sign on the fence announcing a luxury residential compound, VERSAILLES DE SHANGHAI, already selling. Of course Ruth was nowhere.

I had kept the old pair of embroidered shoes back from the auction, the shoes that were found with the manuscript, Yun's shoes, presumably, that matched Ruth's identically. Those shoes were missing too, I realized when I went to lay my hands on them. That was a sign to me that Ruth had really gone. When I stopped rushing about madly and came to my senses, I accepted what I should have known all along. I would not be able to bring her back this time. She had gone.

❋ ❋ I sought the help of Old Weng, who made some inquiries on my behalf. From him I heard that she had returned to Tianzhou, staying overnight with Mrs. Ma in our old inn, before going to the temple to consult Broken Gate, the head monk. Yun received her summons from the barefoot nun who was sweeping the floor of the Hall of Guanyin. So Ruth had received her summons from Han, in their last sighting of each other, without exchanging a word. The bare reminder was enough. She had her own debt to repay, her own path to go. With the coming to light of the true story, she realized that her turn had come to follow her own truth.

We had hung on as long as we could, each of us, tenaciously, with all our human longing. We had returned to the world to complete our story. Now was the time for us to be released at last. The current of feeling between us that joined us to the pulse of life itself had survived all the cycles of our restless roaming. Now was the time to cut the thread.

Broken Gate saw that Ruth understood this thoroughly so he was willing to help with her request. He arranged for her to travel farther inland, up into the mountains, around Jiuhuashan, I believe, where there is a temple that provided her with a temporary home. She moved on again then, apparently, farther into those clouded peaks and misty valleys where time and the world dissolve. That's where she disappeared at last.

Perhaps I knew as well as she did what the ending of our story must be. Only I had kicked against it, as I must, as a man bound by love.

Ruth's father wrote expressing his thanks that I had called him off, since there was to be no operation, and extending his sympathy that his daughter and I were no longer together. He sent his and Laura's warm regards. Later he sent me a postcard he got from Ruth. It was a picture of a gilded elephant in the courtyard of an obscure and plain-looking temple high up in the snows. Ruth wrote that she was dividing her time between her devotions, her needlework, and the kitchen garden. She did not know what would come next. She wrote that her loved ones were often in her thoughts and she wanted us to suffer no sorrow on her account. *And so on to no suffering, cause of suffering, cessation.* Those few words from the Heart Sutra were the only clue she gave about her health. I prayed that her sickness had not returned.

She wrote to her father that she was trying to find time to write a record of the experiences she had undergone, a *seventh* chapter of her own, which she hoped to finish one day soon and send to me. She was playing a joke on me, giving me yet another missing chapter to seek. But I have not received it so far.

Among the things Ruth left behind, intentionally or otherwise, was the semicircle of broken jade. I found it on the bed with the strip of red cloth that had served to tie together Yun's embroidered shoes and Shen Fu's hidden manuscript. It is a reminder of all that happened, one that I treasure as the red thread of my fortune in this world of flesh and dust. It may not be much to show, but it means everything to me.

The complete *Six Chapters of a Floating Life* is soon to be published in a scholarly edition in Taiwan.

A swank new hotel has gone up across the street from my office with a frontage of luxury shops, including one that sells antiques. From my desk at certain times of day I can look way down and observe transactions. I have good eyes. One day I saw a man in tennis whites and a racquet strolling along the pavement. He was elderly, an American I guessed, one of those tanned and muscly gents who push themselves into too much exercise in order to stay virile. He stopped and looked in the window of the antique store at two little *doucai* stem-cups that caught his attention.

I could see what they were from so far away because I already knew they were there, and with quite a price tag on them. They had just turned up there one day. I suppose I regarded them as a kind of trap that this tennis-playing senior was falling into.

Just at the same time, on that particular day, a young woman was passing by. She was well dressed in a tailored jacket and trousers in the best designer black and gray. She might almost have been a young man with her short hair and fashionable dark glasses, except she had a good figure up top.

That's how I picked her as Han. The sight of those wine cups stopped her in her tracks and she pressed against the glass. She had seen them before, of course. She must have recognized them. They would have stood out anywhere, that exquisite pair of imperial Ming stem-cups. Then she noticed the foreign man. That's the sequence in which it happened, so I surmise, and it was inevitable, once their gazes strayed from admiring the porcelain to the intriguing reflection of themselves in the glass, that they would be drawn to each other.

I heard later that Han married a sprightly American movie tycoon and moved to Hollywood. The man died happily of a heart attack six months after the wedding and left Han the China franchise for all the titles his production company owned.

Han has since returned to live in Shanghai, a rich and fortunate woman now. After so long, she is released, and our paths have not crossed, even though we have probably passed through the same lobbies a dozen times.

As to the departure of my beloved, I can only say that in pain there can also be the purest happiness. More than memory, it is the certain knowledge that an experience continues to exist, as it happened, in all its subtle substance, for all time. I ask no more than that.

Once again I am thrown into life's mad turmoil, a floating dream from which I do not know when I shall wake up.

Acknowledgments

For the Chinese original of Shen Fu's memoir, written in 1808 and published without the final two chapters in 1877, I have used the edition compiled by Wang Yiting, *Shen Fu San Wen Xuan Ji* (*Selected Prose of Shen Fu,* Baihua Arts Publishing House, Tianjin, 1997). My adaptation is based on my own translation from the Chinese and Lin Yutang's classic translation, *Six Chapters of a Floating Life,* first published in Shanghai in 1935–36. For the passages from Lin Yutang's translation, used in whole or in part, I am deeply grateful for the cooperation of Taiyi Lin Lai and Hsiang Ju Lin, daughters of the late Lin Yutang. The final two chapters remain missing.

I owe a special debt of gratitude to my friend Alex Kerr for introducing me to *Six Chapters* when we were students and for generously sharing his passion for the book since then. I would also like to thank Wang Ziyin, for her vision of taking it further; Bob Wyatt, for showing me how to do so; Chong Weng-ho for making introductions; and Jay Schaefer, for his painstaking and sensitive editing; my agents, Rosemary Creswell and Derek Johns; Jon Riley in London and Julie Pinkham in Melbourne for their support; Ivor Indyk in Sydney for comments on the manuscript; and all those, too many to mention, who contributed to the book in ways large or small. I gratefully acknowledge the assistance of a Senior Fellowship from the Literature Fund of the Australia Council, the Australian government's arts-funding body.